THE POOR

THE POOR

A NOVEL

By Raul Brandão

Translated by
Karen C. Sherwood Sotelino

DALKEY ARCHIVE PRESS

First published in Portuguese as *Os Pobres* in 1908.

Translation copyright © 2016 Karen C. Sherwood Sotelino

LIBRARY OF CONGRESS CATALOGING-IN-PUBLICATION DATA

Names: Brandao, Raul, 1867-1930, author. | Sotelino, Karen C. Sherwood, translator.
Title: The poor / by Raul Brandao ; translated by Karen C. Sherwood Sotelino.
Other titles: Os Pobres. English
Description: Fird edition. | Victoria, TX : Dalkey Archive Press, 2016. | "Orignially published in Portuguese as Os Pobres in 1908" -- Verso title page.
Identifiers: LCCN 2015045597 | ISBN 9781564787644 (pbk. : alk. paper)
Subjects: LCSH: Poor--Fiction. | Portugal--Fiction.
Classification: LCC PQ9261.B7 P6313 2016 | DDC 869.8/4109--dc23
LC record available at http://lccn.loc.gov/2015045597

Partially funded by a grant by the Illinois Arts Council, a state agency

The book is financed through the Gregory Rabassa Translation Fellowship granted by the Fundação Luso-Americana.

Dalkey Archive Press publications are, in part, made possible through the support of the University of Houston-Victoria and its program in creative writing, publishing, and translation.

Dalkey Archive Press
Victoria, TX / McLean, IL / London / Dublin

Printed on permanent/durable acid-free paper

Table of Contents

Translator's Introduction

The translation of *The Poor* was challenging and rewarding in equal measure. Starting in the opening paragraphs in which Raul Brandão—like some sort of Poseidon—creates a deluge of language and images, through the closing passages in which carefully constructed sentences meander between personifying objects and objectifying human emotion, the exquisite blending of form and content is the Portuguese language at its most expressive. It is a highly innovative novel for 1906, the year it was first published, and one that pushed my imagination to the limit as I read passages in the original and conjured up heretofore unknown combinations of words and images.

> Oh, nightfall, soaked in moonlight, when you can hear the tears of still waterwheels, buckets dropping one by one onto the parched earth, and you can sense the dreamlike dialogues amongst the wild pines . . . And the Tree, in reaction to this noise, is made dizzy, shaken to the very depth of its roots. (73)

The Poor is sparse on traditional descriptions of characters and surroundings; action occurs inside an imaginary world. The narrative develops around the observations, worries, and doubts of the characters, very much like what Virginia Woolf began doing in the 1920s in *To the Lighthouse*, *Orlando*, and *The Waves*.

The overwhelming atmosphere of the deluge at the start of the novel creates in readers the sensation of the rushing murky waters, and they too are drawn into that troubled world. With the first rain, "like a mysterious wave rolling in from some unknown ocean," the author blends human experience with Nature. He does this in part through semantic slippage achieved with the use of the implicit subject (recalling), inserting human emotion into a lengthy description of the rushing water: "A sweet sound, that of the rain. Recalling so many things, lost and sad!" (3) He bestows beauty on the inanimate—"the rocks are left glistening," as if they had just emerged from a luxurious bath—and provides the river with agency and emotion:

> It plows through the earth, exposing roots, dragging humus through the deluge along with dried leaves, dead animals, rocky dregs all swirling together, then dissolving, stirring into the foamy water, headed to the unknown . . . Such is life. A river of moaning, tears, and mystery. (3)

The lack of chronology and spatial references means that readers emotionally absorb rather than intellectually comprehend characters and situation. The translation then, to a certain extent, is emotion- rather than logic-based. One of the main characters, Gebo, initially seems to be a slovenly mess of a man, apparently without sentiment or intelligence. Instead, as the novel progresses, he is revealed as a victim of the economic situation in Portugal—a man with the capacity to search tirelessly for work day after day, and to love his daughter and wife with tenderness and constancy. Because of the gradual and impressionistic revelation of this character, I revisited certain adjectives I had used for him at the beginning of the novel. By exposing Gebo so gently, Raul Brandão makes him emerge from a homogenous mass of the destitute, mirroring the experience of spending time among the poor, learning their stories, and appreciating the contours of their individual personalities.

The personification of emotions—"It isn't hatred she feels for me, because her smile, which I sense damp with tears, is sad, yet resigned. Nonetheless, regret awakens, regret sets to growling . . ." (73)—requires constant vigilance. Since these are innovative images, the usage in English must also be unusual. The unusual imagery begs for time: time spent on translation, time spent on editing, and, certainly, time devoted to reading. Here again, form joins content, because the subject matter, the attempt to comprehend the dispossessed and the importance of the natural environment, also demand our time.

> After death, matter goes into an ocean. Rivers carry the molecules, until they meet up with those they are meant to join. My heart joined to yours will grow into a simple thorn bush. It will be in some modest place, but any passersby this April will be forever moved. My brain will seek out yours to float together in the serenity of some river. Whether on earth or in rocks, I will look for you unconsciously till I find and enjoy you in this stormy ocean. And if you are a fountain, I'll discover you and together we will quench the thirst of many a forgotten root. (75)

While proper names often involve complex translation decisions, Raul Brandão, underscoring his deterministic worldview, names some of his characters with nouns and adjectives. Some of these were easily translated: Corsair, Astronomer, the Dead Man; others, far more complex: "Gebo" is both a noun (tramp, slob) and adjective (slovenly, hunchbacked). Gabiru too is both noun (scoundrel, rascal, old man) and adjective (clumsy). "Look at him . . . Do you know what they call him? They call him Gabiru." (79) As described by literary critic Álvaro Cardoso Gomes, they are personae, not exactly persons; they are spiritual representations that navigate an imprecise universe, wandering around and dreaming vague inner conflicts. As spiritual representations, they are masklike: "From his dormer window he would spend hours pondering this sliver of a girl, virtually consumptive, who seemingly wore a mask on the verge of an anguished cry." (77) To further complicate the situation, at times there is an overlap of identity, as in the case of the Masked Man, the philosopher, and Gabiru. And occasionally names are altered: during the conversation between Gabiru and Pita in chapter 17, instead of using the shortened name "Pita," the character's full name "Pythagoras," is used for the first time. (For clarity, I opted to maintain the shortened version, Pita, used throughout the novel.)

How to keep the novel dreamlike and poetic? This is the subliminal aspect of this novel; the poetic prose lures the reader into the depths of his or her imagination. The author both personifies nature and objectifies the characters, who frequently speak in surreal, stilted language, forming snippets of dialogue and stray comments that seemingly float through the wind. Tone of voice and mood—anger, sorrow, melancholy—must often be guessed.

"Anyone born into this life might as well be dead."
"And what about you? How did you end up here?"
"It was my fate." And the old lady added, "You'll be hungry, you know, and you'll have only . . ."
"What?" says one of them anxiously.
"Stones." (18)

The description of the storm opening the novel is a roaring, rushing metaphor for the terrifying, dangerous state of society. The final image of the novel is of the wooden bench in front of the hospital where everyone—small and great, rich and poor—eventually comes to sit and await death. Although a delicate maneuver to render into English, it comes as barely a surprise when this bench gradually begins speaking nostalgically about having once been a tree, and about the forest it misses so dearly. The novel demands the same recognition of the poor as it does of the nature surrounding them and invading the port city where they live. Raul Brandão's genius was to draw on the fundamental connection between humans and nature, and to decry the inability of society to provide the equally fundamental care for the poor and the environment.

Karen C. Sherwood Sotelino

THE POOR

I
THE DELUGE

WINTER'S COMING. ROCKY hillsides, naked trees—all of nature's enveloped in a stifling, seeping cloud. It's as if everything were withdrawn and brooding.

Like a mysterious wave rolling in from some unknown ocean, it begins to rain. A sweet sound, that of the rain. Recalling so many things, lost and sad! At first the soaked earth swells, and when it bursts there's a rush so torrential, the rocks are left glistening. It plows through the earth, exposing roots, dragging humus through the deluge along with dried leaves, dead animals, rocky dregs all swirling together, then dissolving, stirring into the foamy water, headed to the unknown.

Such is life. A river of moaning, tears, and mystery. A murky wave exposes the deepest roots, as a torrential rush engulfs all disgrace and laughter, relentlessly dragging this human humus up to some shore, where the filthy hands of the suffering finally find another helping hand; where their exhausted, tearful eyes are amazed before an eternal dawn, and where dreams are made real . . .

*   *   *   *   *

Look . . . nightfall. The wind picks up and the passing gust carries cries, catastrophes, and wailing. I'm poor and wary, and know nothing of life, but I'm a prince. You might ask of which land? "Of dreams." And so I live alone, miserable in this building, in this wreckage, listening . . . I hear a river that no one else even senses. There's a spring inside every living creature, a

3

trickle of water carving damp cracks into rocks, or else flowing rashly, torrentially. These springs relieve the drought of life. In some poor, simple creatures the flowing water is faintly audible and . . . so gentle, we're drawn into its shadows. It's emotion. Dig deeper, don't let it dry up: otherwise life itself perishes, like parched earth.

You can always hear the sound of the flooding from inside my tenement; constantly flowing, as is the way of unruly, splendid torrents. Listen . . . ! The fierce Winter speaks, the wind and rains gush, but listen, listen . . . !

*   *   *   *   *

It's my neighbors, the whores downstairs, the two couples next door, and a lost soul they call Senhor José, who lives in the garret. Sometimes the women walk by in the street, their purple shawls trailing behind; the lost soul only goes out at dusk, same as the bats. He's a pallbearer, and even more reticent than I am. I meet him in the stairwell sometimes, coughing through his hoarse, raspy chest.

Why were these outcasts born? They wake up defeated, to scrounge, to cry out for scraps of bread, to rest again only in their graves. A dreamless road, that's their bitter lot: fatigue, humiliation, and hunger.

If they happen to walk by trees on a Spring day—so beautiful that the apple trees, in their enthusiasm, begin revealing their blooms—do you know what happens? The trees recoil, everything falls silent, watching them go by drenched in sweat, browbeaten, and spent. Why do they live on, bellowing, shunned, the riffraff, rocks, and toads? Why does God create them?

*   *   *   *   *

The pallbearer . . . there he is, climbing. Each step reminds me of a shovel of dirt. He's a gloomy, scrawny man carrying his top hat wrapped in his snuff handkerchief and his frock coat folded over his arm. He never talks. I'd venture to say he doesn't even think; he's just a phantom, who leaves home only to go to funerals. He must be evil, he must be callous: one thing's certain, he's never cried. Boys throw rocks at him as he walks down the street, gaunt, cross-eyed, with his top hat and coat; he's the harsh clown of death who, instead of laughter, has heard only tears his entire life. I'd wager he laughs to himself at people sobbing, as coffins are dragged from their homes, like hearts dragged from the living—the laughter of a man tired of being alone, distant, and humiliated . . . Pallbearer! Pallbearer! He survives on tears, thrives on pain. And when he goes out with his torch, ambling lankily behind the funeral car in his shabby masquerade, whatever can he be thinking, sad and gasping . . . ?

*   *   *   *   *

There are others . . . married long ago. They call her Rata. Poor and motherless, she finally got sent to an orphanage, where she grew up. They laugh at her, no more than an abortion, raised through charity. She's spent her life in the infirmary among doctors who spared her from death—intentionally, I think—so she could go on suffering.

I meet her on the stairs, she's wearing man's boots, with tattered elbows, and so skinny and disheveled she's pitiful.

"The best time of my life was the infirmary. The Sister would kiss and caress me . . ."

Stray dogs are happier, and trees, incomparably so.

Her man beats her. He gets home and slaps her, knocks her around. If she cries or complains, he beats her even more. And since she doesn't say anything anymore, only thinks to herself, "I'd be better off a servant!" he wants to make Rata scream and cry.

"You'd be better off a whore, I tell you . . . !"

This morning she appeared with swollen eyes and bruises on

her face. Her dress is ill-fitting and I've noticed since it's been cold she's wearing her husband's shoes on her sockless purple feet. Learn from life, suffer! There's nothing for it. Till death finishes you off with his beatings. Sometimes, if he leaves, she looks out the window, brooding over the Sister who'd kiss and caress her when she got sick—and she asks herself, "So why didn't I die then?"

Shut up and suffer. Till death, till your poor body drops exhausted and broken, black and blue from the beatings. That's the way it'll always be, irremediably, inexorably.

*   *   *   *   *

The old man, fat and flaccid, pausing on the stair landing with his disheveled white hair, is Gebo. He's hunchbacked, and his watery eyes stare blankly.

"Gebo!"

Lifting his big, anxious face, he answers "Uh . . . ?"

There are others like him. A constant human deluge, torrentially polishing the rocks. The gusty wind thrashes the tenement and moves past, sweeping up the fretful moans and dust, carrying them off to some other strange world. And with nightfall, life intensifies. It's a horde of muck, of people who've torn away their masks: some men are dreams, you might say others are cries. Gebo settles in to tell his story and a tragic old woman, called Corsair, appears with her white clown-face; so too the Astronomer, a hairy wise man; and also the slender philosopher Gabiru, who's as stiff as a board, and has discovered worlds, yet doesn't know the simplest things in life. He stirs the embers of his ideas and he's never looked life in the face. He walks down the streets astonished, like a navigator at his ship's bow, lost in a world he's discovered. And, down below in the basement, there lives—for how many years?—*the Masked Man*, whose story nobody knows. He's shut himself away. He hates light, that blue dust seeping through everyone and everything, through March, and through trees. He no longer sees life, turbulent and wide as a river. He's alive, but inside a tomb: only the walls—ablaze with his dreams, and deep crimson like the walls of a forge—know his past. Gebo stops on the landing, telling his woes to anyone among the poor willing to listen. Several gather around and, ridiculously, he breaks down in tears as he narrates his sad existence of humiliation and begging, gasping for breath, cast aside, his needy daughter, the world's scorn, his crazed, tearful ramblings in search of bread for his family.

And he always ends with, "I regret I've been so honest . . ."

*   *   *   *   *

The foreboding wind picks up, shaking the Tenement. What's a house made of? Stone. The entire globe is turned inside out to house man. Trees and the bones of the earth are torn out to serve him. Then add cries. Stones, trees, and cries have made the Tenement. Add dreams, transforming everything. One person screams from underground, and another, through so much dreaming, has covered the black granite in gold dust. So the entire house, battered and ravaged, has taken on the appearance of those lives. It's Gebo's house, and the prostitutes', and Gabiru's, and Pita's. The front door is wide open, the roof tiles are falling off; but when the dilapidated dormers way up high shield the sun, you believe the Tenement's meditating, and singing. Yes, indeed, it's made of stone . . . and dreams.

It's raining, but the arid earth has neither water nor plants.

Just one tree grows in that barren soil. Nourished on sorrow. Its roots have dug all the way through to the hospital, built opposite the Tenements to suck the life from the poor. When moonbeams filtered through the clouds reach that tree—then we see only its ghost, made entirely of moonlit dust.

I stay by myself on these long nights, listening to the live deluge. It's often tears flowing or emotions gushing at the sound of a trickle from a spout of glistening murmurs. The tears are always made up of peaceful sorrow . . . In the black night, the Hospital walls off the city from trees, damp waterwheels refresh the earth, and solitary hillsides seemingly ban the desperate. It's like an ancient stone moat, filled with heaps of live coals, lying in wait for the suffering: the saintly, the poor, the fallen women, and the heroes.

Pita, wrapped in his blanket-cape, sometimes murmurs as he contemplates the hospital, "These castles are built of human charity, so the rich never have to see the suffering of the poor. And they're made of stone and solid granite, so the screams cannot be heard from outside."

II
GEBO

You must have seen him, a fat old fellow, with disheveled white hair and so fretful he's the source of both laughter and pity. Sometimes he stumbles in the street, rights himself, then, all muddied, he looks around and sobs. And he keeps walking, wheezing. It seems as if he's about to scream, this flaccid, fat fellow with disheveled white hair, when suddenly, quietly he asks for spare change. He laughs, humiliated, and trembles like a sack of blubber, with disheveled white hair. It's Gebo—a hobo because he's ludicrous and shabby, and ridiculous because hard luck has beaten him so far down.

*　　*　　*　　*　　*

A sad existence, with no hatred, and no screams. He didn't understand it . . . life, and he took every knock with the surprised anguish of the bewildered. Whatever had he done wrong? What? So, is hardship laughable? Is suffering laughable?

And all around him mouths were agape, at seeing him there, fat, begging, grotesque.

The worst part of ruin can be summarized with this harsh sentence—to be unhappy. Some people are born under a sign—to suffer through life. Everything would go wrong for Gebo, even the simplest, most insignificant things, things that barely exist for others. Then, dumfounded and dazed, he'd stop and wonder at his bad luck. What had he done to suffer so?

Besides his bad luck, Gebo had always been ludicrous. Some people go through life thus, knowing neither suffering nor kindness, without a trace, just like the hidden water veins that sustain the earth.

Even when he sobbed, his mask and his disheveled white hair made people laugh.

Though constantly sweating, barely able to yell or complain, Gebo had a fiery heart. He was one of those types rendered even more ridiculous for having been victim to all sorts of disasters: ruin, misery, and hunger. The whole world slinging mud at him, and off he goes, resigned and weeping . . .

"Hey, Gebo!"

Everyone would laugh at his anxious blubbering. Some would say, "If only he weren't such a fool!" And the poor, whom he had so often helped, relished seeing him humbled and trod upon, like a dirt road. So tell me, why do we find consolation in others' misfortune?

Sweating along anxiously, downtrodden, forty years of age, that flaccid, fat fellow still believed in life, just like trees and children do.

At which dank, disastrous moment did he meet up with the bad luck that never left his side? Ruin wraps itself around the neck of some people and remains there forever! For a lifetime! Never lets go. Loss and suffering set in—worse than the darkest thoughts anyone could harbor. They'd deceive him, happy to see him downtrodden and lost, a shove here, another there, and he'd stumble his way through this world.

Gebo was married, and had this one good fortune: a daughter. Ah, a daughter! A daughter always breathes life into a man! A little girl always holds such strength in her tiny hands! And so this ridiculous, fat old man had once known happiness. It was one of those dim homes, hidden away, where life flows with the monotony of a spring, always ready to quench every thirsty mouth. A little old house, a small garden with six trees, a rustling creek, and windows opening onto the friendly shadows of the fruit trees. Contentment was there. Trees provide all their shade, they never disappoint.

*   *   *   *   *

For a long time he lied to his wife, who lived in ignorance. Gebo
would laugh, his heart wrenched, just so they'd have a few more
hours of happiness—the last hours before their ruin. Until one
day, he succumbed.

"I didn't want to tell you . . . but, woman . . . oh,
woman . . . !"

"What? What happened?"

"All's lost, all's lost . . ."

"Lost?!"

"Yes, all's lost . . . And now? Now? Nobody helps me,
nobody cares. I've asked, I've searched . . . I can't go on! All's
lost, woman . . ."

"All is lost?"

"Yes . . ."

"It's your fault, you're not at all clever. Everyone laughs at
you. Everyone fools you and on top of that, they laugh at you.
Go on, get out . . . ! What do you expect? What's going to happen to me and the little one? Are we to blame for your foolish-
ness, your bad luck . . . ?"

"No, no, woman, I know . . ."

"Get going!"

And he'd go back to his grind, rambling around daily,
wheezing, until one night his wife saw him come in, hatless
and muddy, exhausted—with his disheveled white hair. Pallid
from all the ingratitude. It was twilight. Defeated, like a sack
of blubber, he was trembling in pain, talking quietly, "Oh, my
little girl . . . ! Everyone laughs at me, everyone . . . Nobody
cares. Who cares about anyone else's hard luck? Oh, my dear
daughter!"

He started to lead a bewildered, crazed life. It seemed as if
everywhere he turned there were voices calling out, ridiculing
him, "Gebo! Hey Gebo!" There was no more peace on earth for

him: even at home he constantly heard his wife's furious repri-
mands and witnessed his daughter's silent tears. Oh, the times
he looked around, lost, and saw only heartlessness and laughter!
Those times had left him in sweaty anguish for the rest of his
days. Everything had been laid to waste. He would collapse
under his wife's words, crushed, with not an ounce of strength
to fight back, broken by disappointment and indifference.

"And now what? Now what?" She'd ask him.

And he, crestfallen, "Now . . . I don't know . . . now we'll
starve to death."

He'd knocked on every door in vain, he was ruined, with
neither ideas nor strength. All he could do was sob, limp and
grotesque, while his wife, hardened by ill-fortune, insulted him,
screaming, "But get up! Go out and look! Save us!"

Get going, Gebo! And he would go back to his friends, begging, confused, asking for loans, extra time, garbling his words,
then suddenly waving his arms and breaking out in cries and
sobs.

You must have met him, this fat old fellow, with his disheveled white hair, shoved through life, his fretful manner the
source of both laughter and pity.

"Hey, Gebo!"

"Huh?"

"What's going on?"

And he'd answer immediately, rushing through the same old
words, swallowing his tears, "Oh, Lord! I've walked so much
and suffered so. No matter what I do, things only get worse,
and worse . . . I just can't take it anymore. All is lost! Only God
knows what I've been through, my ruin, my anguish just to
come by one measly crumb to put in our mouths . . . It's worse
for them. My heart's breaking, that's how much I've suffered.
I've got the darkness of the night inside me. What's to be done?
Relish the ruin? Huh? I regret I've been so honest . . ."

And there he'd be, sobbing, with his sagging mouth and his
disheveled white hair.

III

THE WOMEN

THE PROSTITUTES START singing at night. Among parched stones and the clamor of voices, the prostitutes start singing. They're poor, disgraced and pitiful, mud created by man, specially for his pleasure. The darkness disperses their ragged melody and carries it away, shreds of soulful sadness, nocturnal, weeping anxiety. Nighttime . . . go forth . . . come hither, regrets, dreams, it's time! From black blocks a City is built. Still, there are sparse clearings, which a mute Shadow, gropingly and suddenly, smothers in silence. And among doors left ajar faces appear. Only remorse can draw those sad, tired expressions that blend into those of the dead.

It's time for the pallbearer to come down, his footfalls echoing in the stairwell, for Gebo to tell his incoherent tales yet again, and for the poor to go out in search of bread.

The women talk in the dark, to forget. Sometimes their mouths disappear and one tragic voice erupts from the depths, as if the darkness itself were speaking. From off in the distance, the night answers, "Hey, you there!"

"What?"

"I just remembered something."

"What?"

"Do you know what the worst thing in life is? It's when you can't even feel sorrow."

"Oh, there you go again . . ." Ever so slowly, nightfall smothers them, and in the darkness they sense the birth of Disgrace . . . They are suddenly silent and then the same voice continues, "One of them wants me laughing; the next wants me sad. What do they care?"

13

"And then what?"

"Nothing. But even so, think about it, it's so sad that we can't even remember . . ."

"Remember what?"

"The past . . ."

"We shouldn't even try."

"I'd rather be dead," says another voice.

"And you?"

"Me? You're talking to me?" asks a scrawny woman emerging from the darkness. "I'd rather have no memory at all, so I'd never see her again laid out in her coffin, the look on her face when she saw me."

"Who?"

"My mother."

"Ah . . . !"

"Yeah . . ." says the first voice, "in this life it's better not to remember. Go back to your singing girls . . . Sing!"

And the women go on with their singing, their ragged melody of enormous sorrow. Then they stop, and one of them starts talking again. They always say the same words, just for the noise, they don't care if anyone listens. One of them laughs at everything. She's skinny, pallid, and worn out. She wears a black patch on one eye and is always laughing at herself, at everyone else, and at all her misfortune as if she were wearing a mask.

"I'm Mouca," she says, giggling. "My mother threw me out when I was a young girl, and me, if I had a daughter, I'd put her out on the streets to start earning her living. The thieves took me in, I grew up in the street and made my bed of stone doorsteps . . . The thieves took me in. Oh, life!"

"Hey, you, aren't you ever going to shut up?"

"When I was a kid, I spent a whole winter in a tattered shirt. As a matter of fact, it did me good, now I never get cold. Besides that, they'd beat me up. Do you know what? They'd kick me for no reason at all. I learned. It was a tough life . . . A thief had me when I was thirteen. A bald old man that looked like Saint

Peter. They used to call him the Slug, you must have heard of
him. You pay the price to learn anything . . . Oh, life! Life! I'm
made of dirt, dirt everyone tramples on, but I've done some
treading of my own, too. Things could be worse, that much I
know. Why, I've seen folks die for want of a scrap of bread. Mind
you, I've known ruin. I've faced it . . . It's no good lowering
yourself . . . Then one day, you end up falling for some fellow
and that's even worse. What's to be done? We've all got to put up
with it, we're all the same, the rich and folks without a drop of
water. The worst is when you end up falling for some fellow . . .

"Do you all know what love is? Love is when you're no more
than a dog. We're worthless and they've got it all. Then you've
got love. He's beating me and I'm saying to myself, 'You beat
me 'cause you like me . . .' That's when you've got love, it's when
we're no more than a dog . . . Me, a slave, him, the master. It's
all over! We've all got to suffer."

"All of us. There's nothing worse than being born woman."

"I never had any luck. What did I care if he beat me? I'd look
over my bruises and tell myself, 'He's my friend.' One day he
broke my arm, but we're just like dogs, we only like masters that
kick us. The worst was when he'd treat me bad. Men are all the
same . . . Oh, life! Life! Then, one day he said, 'I'm sick of you.'
And, you know what? He never spoke to me again. Oh! The
more you suffer for a man, the more you want him! 'But, just let
me love you . . . !' And he'd say, 'Go on, get out!' I thought I'd
die. Drank all day long just to trouble the pain that'd set into
my heart. But he'll be back! He'll be back! Ah, never!"

"What was his name?"

"What do you care? No good bringing back the dead. Let
sleeping dogs lie. And if you'd only seen him dead, like I did!
Seeing the dead body of someone you've held in your arms, it's
like seeing your child in a coffin. You can scream all you want
and they don't come back to life! I never got over him . . . So,
once I got myself all dolled up and just as cool as a corpse, I
went to have a word with him: 'What do you want?' he said. And

I said, 'I want to serve you.' And I laughed. 'I know you can't stand the sight of me, it's over! I don't care. All I ask is to serve you. I've come to be your servant.' He started laughing. Then she came in and I laughed even more. 'I've come here to be your maid, how much yer gonna pay?' They started whispering. 'I'll kiss the ground you walk on. Here I am, at your service.' They kept laughing at me. 'On your way, slave!' I was still giggling, 'I'll do whatever you want!' 'Make yourself scarce, slave!' and I started on my way. So one day I up and put arsenic in their food. They ate it. And when I saw him there dead, I really split my sides laughing. They carried me off. In jail, they had me in for questioning and I just snickered. My cheeks hurt, I laughed so hard, and I kept seeing him, right there next to me, dead. 'Why did you kill him?' And I'd just snicker . . . So there you have it, everyone has their fate. We've all got to bear it and we've all got to suffer. I'm Mouca." And she finished off in gales of laughter.

*   *   *   *   *

Their doorway, open to tragedy and torment, is opposite the Hospital. The wives of thieves and soldiers, living next door to pain. The walls are black and damp: hands have scratched them, filled them with anguish, and screams have left them shaken. You would think they had been built from the same dream, the same stone from which life is made.

Inside, in the smoky, oily lighting, the women expose them-selves like used rags, or like masks. You might say they're like portraits drawn in sweating sorrow, there is so much despera-tion in those chortling mouths. Two of them peek from behind the door, one of them stares fixedly with a petrified expression, doused in pain, another sings while their toothless, fat madam calculates her profits. She's tough and pompous, with a cruel expression and a short temper. Sometimes she preaches at them for hours on end, "Love tastes bitter. Worse than death . . . Don't you want it, you all hear me?"

"Ma'am, how you carry on! Real sorrow's finding yourself all alone in this world," says one beaten down, consumptive woman.

"To have what? Scorn, that's about it," adds another.

"As for me, if I was all alone in this world, I think I'd go drown myself."

"So, get moving! Get moving! Have your fill of disgrace. Have your fill, that's all there is. Who are you, anyway? Less than dirt . . . You'll leave this earth filled with disgrace. You're better off dead in the river!"

"As for me," says another, "my body's black and blue but what do I care? I'd rather be dead than have my man walk out on me . . . For my own salvation, I'd head straight for the river."

"And then you complain . . ." the old woman threatens, "you're worse off than the whores."

"My man's beatings don't even hurt me, and what's more, he made me eat dirt," swears another.

"We don't have one single person in this world. Who wants to have anything to do with a *wretch*?"

"We've got no father, no mother, not one living soul."

"If I cry, everyone else laughs. What does anyone care?"

"And no one in the world should cry alone . . ."

"As for me," says Mouca, "I'm so used to them paying me, if my fellow stays the night, I hide coins in the sheets . . . when I wake up, I find them, just like if someone'd paid."

The others snicker and their madam admonishes, "Don't you see . . . ? Look what happened to Maria! She drowned herself and her lover's there laughing. Helia ended up in the hospital. And she's dead. And you'll all die, if you give in to your heart."

"Sometimes you're better off dead."

"Dead!" says the consumptive girl.

"I tried to kill myself once . . . And then what? I was all alone in this world, he'd booted me out. So I went and drank a big glass of rum, stirred with match sticks. You think I'm sorry? Oh, Ma'am, if you only knew what it feels like . . . ! When she came and told me—it was Mouca—that my man'd taken up with

another woman, it was like I was seeing my own mother rise up
before me—whom I'd killed, drowned in her own tears, shed
over my wicked life. I couldn't even scream. All my screaming
dried up, right here in my throat. I went out, wandered around.

"Her door was closed and I stayed out there in the cold till
morning. Men walking by said whatever they felt like, 'cause no
one knows what goes on in someone else's heart. I felt sorry for
myself, spent the whole night either moping or sobbing. That
day he beat me all over, bruised and black as the scarf 'round
my head. Look . . . I still have the scars. I'll take them to my
grave. 'Have your fill, if you must, but don't leave me . . .' 'Get
going,' he said, 'get out of here, bitch, I can't stand the sight of
you.' And to think . . . ! If that's how life is, if that's what we're
here for, to be tossed out . . . if there's no more to it, we're better
off dead. I should have died, put an end to this suffering . . ."

"The hospital's right there waiting for you, girls," says the
madam, from off in the corner.

"I've heard the students cut us up for learning . . . ?"

"And what do I care?"

"I heard about it once, from one of them . . . and how they
all laugh about it."

"Once we're dead, we don't feel anything anyway."

"I think the poor always go to the students, so they can
learn."

"Well, what makes me sad . . . is to think of my poor body,
all cut up in pieces!"

"The hospital's just right across the way, waiting for you,
girls . . ."

"Can't you just shut up?"

They laugh, one of them starts sulking and the madam continues, "My dears, you can still get rich. What you need is a lot
of experience in life. Mark my words, there's no more to life than
suffering and vanity. There's nothing worse than growing old in
poverty . . . Everyone laughs! You ask for bread, they give you
scorn. They even laugh at our hatred, do you hear me?"

"Anyone born into this life might as well be dead."

"And what about you? How did you end up here?"

"It was my fate." And the old lady adds, "You'll be hungry, you know, and you'll have only . . ."

"What?" says one of them anxiously.

"Stones."

"It's all over!" says another, brooding.

"We'd be better off dead."

"Better off."

"Get moving, get moving! The hospital's there waiting. You'll have everything you need there, a cot and sheets. And there's always room for us at the cemetery. It's never full."

"It's always hungry," murmurs a girl, smiling.

"Yeah," her companion agrees.

"Well, it can have us!" exclaims Mouca.

"Grow old, poor, and you'll see! You'll see!" the madam threatens, standing up.

"What, Ma'am?"

"Forever . . . there's always a stone in your heart, it's always there, you can't tear it out."

"So why are we born? Just to suffer?" asks Sofia.

"That's right. We've come into this world to suffer."

"Oh, no . . . !"

"You're all wrong. You have to save up, hoard your money. Everything else is just for show . . ."

But one of the girls speaks up, the sad, scrawny consumptive. "Everyone despises us in this life, so we have to find at least one person, someone as poor as we are . . ."

"Even if he's a thief . . ." interrupts Luísa.

"Gotta be with a fellow that doesn't make us feel bad."

"We got ourselves into this sad life and we'll never get out," another insists. "Believe me, I remember . . . Everyone here is less than nothing, just dirt."

* * * * *

Either they're quiet and brooding or else they spend the long winter nights singing, opposite the tragic hospital. During the day, when the door's wide open, you can see the hospital bench. There's nothing that aches more than those miserable planks of dried, worn-out pinewood, and nothing more moving. They're alive, they tremble. Some things, for having been so often touched by human hands, take on a soul, a face. Bodies have slumped there near death, bodies that pain has bored into like a drill. Those dried-up planks have taken on a new existence for constantly feeling the scratching of desperate, drowning hands (everyone entering the hospital spends time there, saints, poets, and the poor, all of them, their mouths filled with screams).

That bench was once a tree, torn from the earth to support the poor. It's even more beautiful now than when it stood tall on a solitary mountain, in the snow, in the sun, beneath storms and stars. Here it is, finally standing up only to pain. Planks of wood that at one time provided forest shade, soaked in sap and blueness, are now the resting place of the miserable: stained in blood, rubbed with suffering, and permeated with the sweat of the ill-fated.

IV
GABIRU

GABIRU LIVES ON the last floor of the tenement. He's a solitary philosopher, slender, as sad as a funeral, and armed with the most formidable and strangest of wisdom in God's creation. He has never really lived. To him, everything beyond the hospital is a huge, unknown green ocean.

Nor does he understand reality. He's always alone; the only thing he and his enormous nose have ever voraciously consumed has been drawn from an overflowing fountain of dreams. He has a critical eye and, settled in the dormer window with his dastardly, heavy volumes, he allows his ideas to flow freely, like rivers. And thus, metaphysical, poor, and of few words, he lies down with Mouca, the soldiers' wretch.

He was born to dream. He sighs with relief as he locks himself away in the garret, crying out, "I'm going to think . . . !" He knows words and theories and has read huge old tomes, yet he's never seen the rivers and mountains before his very eyes, nor the trees. He delves into profound ideas and has never known reality.

And so he is both happy and sorrowful. At the window of his cubicle, he senses the golden gushing of days; he concentrates on some wondrous dream and he loves. And then, from among his woven ideas, he emerges, a tragic figure, laughing daily along with thieves and soldiers.

But life means nothing to him. Although something immaterial does exist—violet, golden emotions—surrounding him, nearly touching him, then suddenly fleeing, hurt and tearful. So thread by thread he carries on, weaving and building his theory:

Ah, how I tremble before trees, before moonbeams flowing palely, silently, before the splendor of nature . . . ! I'm taken for a fool when in fact I nearly scream in fear as I behold the amazing universe. Look inside the darkness and listen to the mystery, water silently spouting, the tree with its arms reaching out, the murky sea.

Men go along indifferently, but I feel myself losing my mind before the simplest of things: a sliver of a cloud, like a streaking shroud, a ray of dusty light falling in my bedroom, all golden and alive. I've never gotten used to looking nature in the eye. This! What does it mean? Is it a dream, a crying out of beauty, a soul? Ethereal green hills, infinite constellations, the mist born from the ocean and flowing over it, like an extraordinary roller, a gigantic ghost . . .

I cannot get used to it. Every morning it's as if I were to find myself before monstrous nature for the first time—gold, green, and blue like her rivers, forests, and roaring oceans. Her trees, like living creatures . . . ! That's why, especially during these winter days when the god Adamastor preaches over this lacerated land in his astonishing voice, I settle in to ponder the enigma, hidden and alone.

*   *   *   *   *

I must, however, admit: I'm unusual. Some even assume I am insane. But everyone like me, made merely of leftover, broken dreams, has this shrunken, pained manner. At this time of night, when the universe seems deserted and when even the sound of pen on paper gives me pause, I withdraw into myself and listen: something, and it's not me, begins to murmur softly. And thus I'm lost, in the corner of the dark dormer window, shrunken and lean, dreaming about what? This infinite beauty, the fiery universe.

I'm no longer used to speaking, but I dream. There are splendorous voices inside me: trees sprout from me, and mutilated statues, living bits of dreams. Ah, I believe each being is made from the souls of mountains, stones, and waters; and I also believe there's a mysterious link between man and these worlds. I'm attached to the stars and to humble thistle.

If I walk by shrunken and lean, they say chortling, "There goes Gabiru!"

Let them say it! I'm far happier than those that ridicule me and I'd rather live among the miserable than with them. They feed the emotions for my dreams. Then I close myself away in this tall garret, built inside the roof tiles, from where I see admirable souls: green flickering flames—and they're trees; clouds resting on the earth, abundantly golden, or else of faint violet—and they're mountains; and lively rolling fluid rushes—and they're rivers. It took me a long time to decipher their names. None among the miserable knew, because the enormous Hospital walls off the city; so this damp life composed of waterwheels, deluge of dregs, trees, Springtime, and cries from the sun remains, unknown to everyone suffering below, amidst the dried granite. Only Pita, in the garret next door, sees as I do the splendor of nature—the Mother.

Ah! And sometimes, a cloud of sunshine falls on terrified things, all of them green, and I nearly touch the mystery. I hear nature's words, in a vast language, and I don't understand the meaning. The sounds are lost syllables, some golden, others green. The air is fine, a soul dusted with moonlight, the trees swoon, and the huge pale mountains—where the sun has scattered soot, gradually fading away as night falls—speak quietly, dizzyingly. Even more timid is the murmuring of the springs, as if they did not want to interrupt the amazing conversation.

This is the best time to listen and it's when I nearly understand the words. Some things are senseless: trees will fall heavy with emotion and from every living thing there emerges an amazing ethereal, living soul, surrounding me, touching me, and speaking! It will speak . . .

Where is all this beauty born? Where does it all come

from . . . ? If a man falls down prostrate, screaming, his fiery words are no more than sounds, which mixed with other cries of pain form the words of a great monologue. And do you really think mountains, eagles, and oceans exist by chance alone, do you believe that . . . ? They're syllables, voices of the Earth in conversation. Worlds and stars are the words of Him who preaches into the infinite. It is always the same force, the only force that creates beauty and dreams, the force whence Life blooms.

I'd perceived that pain has always been necessary in producing things of beauty, of greatness, so that we're able to capture a piece of a barely glimpsed, fleeting dream, so that our squalid hands can grasp a scrap of this amazing being. So that life has meaning, which is to love and to create, and so that something permanent is left behind. Within every cry, beauty thrives. Material things are born from the grave, shapes, trees, and clouds—absolute beauty flows from pain.

"And to what end?" you'll inquire.

Consider a sculptor: to carve a marble figure, to realize the vision only glimpsed, he has to suffer. Then he thrashes out the clay, petrifies the pain. And what if the clay were to suffer? Thus God crushes the clay of which we're made, in order to build extraordinary things: worlds, Life and Death, the infinite soul through which everything flows.

What do poets need in order to create a work of genius? Pain. To suffer is to create. Do you recall those marble figures, forever bent over antique tombs? The moonlight renders them dreamlike as it shines on them through the gothic rose window, renders them dust. They tremble; one could say they take flight. And so, thread by thread, pain gives life to dreams, like moonlight.

To create, one must suffer. It has always been true and remains so, only pain gives life to inanimate things. With a chisel and an inert tree trunk, wondrous works are created, if the sculptor has suffered. Furthermore, with words and lost sounds, with immaterial objects another miracle is possible: to make laughter and dreams, to cause the shedding of tears among other creatures. With the simple, dry letters of the alphabet, some miserable person of genius, immersed in hidden water, builds something eternal, more beautiful and solid than if materials were wrenched from the heart of mountains.

What then is pain, which extraordinary miracle enables it to instill life in stone? What is this terrifying fluid that communicates, the soul wrenched from the soul itself and divisible, like bread? Never under the sun has a person suffered true pain, pain whose suffering has not ultimately served as consolation or savior. Even the most humble, such as dried and withered trees, eventually illuminate and give warmth to the poor.

Pain instills life, but is not life itself: it creates and converts amazing works, and nothing else communicates, persuades, makes brothers of men in the same way . . . After all, to where do all these cries, unified into one great wail, go? If nothing is lost, what does this deluge of tears in the universe sustain? God?

For a long time I listened to the sound of voices, of exasperation, of crying out. It came from the war, the Hospital, from human misery.

And from this trampled ocean flashes of lightning are born, stirred up clouds from where worlds emerge. This eternal world of screaming, flowing since the birth of man, will gush into infinity.

Pain is the only true force that creates and destroys: it is the Force. It feeds God and slime. Pain is an ocean of flames, the spirit of the universe, creating brightness in the soul of the disgraced and giving birth to mountains.

*   *   *   *   *

Trees are the emotion of life.

*   *   *   *   *

Dream! Suffer!

*   *   *   *   *

This world is perhaps, as an unknown philosopher once said, a
drop of water from an ocean of infinite beauty.
The universe is the painful dream of God.

*   *   *   *   *

Nothing is lost. The soul, ideas, emotions are all part of the
force that causes both the sky and the humble, unseen orchards
to bloom.

*   *   *   *   *

I collect pain. I spend my life collecting tatters from this flaming
blanket.
The world is mysterious, filled with cries. Every step of the
way there is a tomb whence some mixture is reborn; a blu-
ish-green, golden dust digs down where the Unknown stirs up
shapes: the ocean, creatures, stones, storms, everything alive and
speaking! Men pass by unaware, but I tremble in fear.
These poor creatures, living in the same building where I live,
thieves, philosophers, gravediggers, and fallen women—all are
crushed so that something may be created. They breed mystery,
the ocean stirred up in pain, and the dwarf apple trees. Under
our indifferent gaze, every step of the way, miracles take place:
the sun, spouting water, and wild, living pine trees.

*   *   *   *   *

Listen . . . things cry. On this cold winter night—windswept—
what won't they say . . . ! They are wracked—it has been raining
for so long . . . The wind tears them apart and it's always sad

to hear the shedding of so many tears. Sometimes they remain there anxiously, as if they were listening or whispering among themselves.

I tremble, and to forget, I set to writing my book, *The Tree*. It is from the mire of these humble things that I build my distorted statue . . . One fine afternoon, imbibing my thoughts, as if in a vast horizon, I didn't notice someone had come in through the slightly open door. So I was startled when I heard a methodical voice next to me, "Philosophical scheming, my illustrious friend . . ."

"What?"

It was Pita, but a transfigured, sad Pita; Pita with fewer teeth and an indescribably sad smile; an older, more sordid Pita.

"Philosophical scheming, my illustrious friend. Reality is sad and bitter. All this you see and do not understand, trees, mountains, and waters, when you get to the bottom of it, it is as stirred up and crushed as human mire. One root comes along and tears up another, one new branch is quick to shove another aside. Each mountain engenders as much hatred as the human heart."

"My friend, have you by any chance ever seen a tree up close? I've only ever seen the one in the entryway."

"Yes, I'm familiar with them, and not only through fine authors, but also for having slept in their fresh, sandy shade . . . They are different, alive and enormous."

"And the ocean?"

"The ocean, which you can see off in the distance, all dusty green, is tragic and ferocious. It roars in wild fury. It is green and filled with rage . . . I am the only one who can give you categorical, real, absolute information at this time, the only one, Pita da Conceição, because in the entire universe, I hold this terrible secret."

"And Mother nature?"

"A mixture, a little cauldron filled with cries; stirred, shredded shapes, mouths unable to scream. Look . . ."

Beyond the hospital there were flickering lights, forgotten

threads of sunlight tangled in the trees, caught in thorny hill-sides. Nevertheless, you could say life was renewed: the pine trees were growing and murmuring, the gurgling sap clung to the tree trunks. The water, of course, would make a more lively sound, and the earth, burned by the sun, would drink it all up in one gulp. The tired waterwheels would yet drop their last beads of sweat, and from the night, gone dark, there erupted a murmur, the voices of the trees, the rivers, and mountains.

"Philosophical scheming, my illustrious friend . . ."

V
GEBO'S STORY

FINALLY, BY THE start of that cold, harsh winter, he had sold off everything, even his daughter's gold. For his being so old and so ludicrous, you might have said he was like a discarded rag, or else an old man with disheveled white hair, talking to himself. Everyone knew him.

"Hey, Gebo!"

"Huh?"

*   *   *   *   *

His wife, who had always been so good, had grown bitter with the poverty. Nervous and withered, she would spend hours upon hours sobbing, huddled in a corner, or cursing her fate all day long, her monologues filled with screaming, trampled dreams, all awash in tears. If only it would all come to an end . . . ! But even Death does not listen to the miserable, nor does time pass quickly. She toils at her grindstone, working her sorrows, afflictions, and black bread.

Every day was exactly the same, somber and sorrowful. There was crying one day, as there was the next; it always looked like rain, as if winter were inescapable.

"So, you've given everything away and lent the rest to all and sundry. And now what? Now what?" his wife would say. "And what's worse, they all laugh at you, and no one helps you. We're starving to death."

"Never mind, woman, never mind. Be patient . . ."

"It's worse for us, for me and the little one."

"I know, that's what worries me. If I were by myself, I could just go off and die!"

"If only you weren't such a fool! Look how your friends get ahead."

"Oh, woman, but what am I supposed to do? Can't you tell me what to do?"

"Just go out and steal! Steal!"

There were dark words, countless woes. Every once in a while, they would forget and set to talking, clinging to some hope that, no sooner born, misfortune would trample. The humblest dust of an illusion was enough for the three of them to settle in together on the cot, freezing with misery, ready to build the most magnificent castles and to forget everything. Only their daughter Sofia was constant. She never complained, and was thin and pretty, with a smile so sad it was like days when the sun shone through the rain.

So, off he would go, beaten down and looking so worried it made people laugh. He looked wrinkled: the scars from his scuffles had never faded.

His wife spent her days in desperate battle against misery, struggling for the last shreds, fighting for each and every one of them, one by one, until they were gone. In the evening, the old man's slow steps and troubled, gasping breaths could be heard on the stairs.

"That's him . . ." she would murmur.

Gebo would come in and she would voraciously vent all she had been mulling over during the course of the day, "You're finally back! So, what's new? Come on! Is there any hope?"

"No, nothing, woman, nothing," and he would sit down, dejectedly.

"No one cares about you, anyway. What are you? Do you know what you are?"

"No, what am I?"

"You're useless. There's not one person that doesn't laugh at you, your bad luck, and the foolish things you've done . . . And, where's all the money we've scrimped and saved?"

"I sure don't know. Let's not talk about it anymore . . . What's done is done . . ."

"That's what you want . . . But I've got to talk and you've got to listen. You've ruined everything, given money to everyone . . . You've got me, you've got the little one. You should have cared, that's what you should have done."

"Oh, come on, woman, you keep repeating the same old story every day. Don't I have enough trouble! What for?"

"What for? For everything!"

At night, by the light of the oil lantern, Gebo did his bookkeeping with his freezing cold hands and a blanket over his shoulders. His daughter, hidden in the shadow, would mend his clothes, and his wife would curse and complain, pacing the room. The lantern would shine on Gebo's oily face, on his huge nose and sad eyes and at the other side of the table Sofia's hands, alone in the glowing light, would work all night long, silently, with no respite.

"I once had such nice handwriting and now . . . grief wears a man out."

"Oh, you poor thing! Poor you! Lots of other people have problems, setbacks, and they get right up again . . ." his wife told him.

"They're lucky, that's all. You need luck for anything," bent over his books counting, he murmured, "and, plus seven . . ."

"Luck! Luck! It's all your fault, you've got no gumption. Go out and look! Quit lolling around . . . all you want to do is eat and sleep."

"Oh, woman . . . !" and he would lift his big, anxious face, the light shining on him directly, his watery eyes in the glow. "Oh, woman, a man gets worn out . . . the same old misery! Always the same old misery . . ."

"Everything goes wrong for us!"

"But . . ."

"Everything. Just leave me alone!"

And she would break down in tears. Then Gebo, nervously rubbing at the sheet of paper, would lie to lift her spirits, "One of these days I'll go into business, you'll see . . . Don't you worry . . . Carry five . . . Besides, our St. Michael's day will come. All this bad luck has got to tire of following us around."

The bread he brought home every day was sheer charity, but from all his lying he had begun to believe his own illusions.

The old woman would cheer up. She would then get up and roam around the room, bundled in her worn shawl. "No, we've got to get out of this mess."

"We will, this time we will, you'll see. I've gotten involved in some deals . . . And, you know what else . . . ? Let me get back to work."

The mother would go lie down and Sofia, silent until then, would say as she stood up, "Don't worry, Father."

"I won't, dear, I won't. It's just her way, poor thing. She's right, she's been through so much. You go off to bed too. Give me a kiss . . . That's a good girl. I'll just do some bookkeeping."

"Good night, Father."

Alone there, Gebo deliberated for a long time, staring at the light. Then, hours and hours later, the pen on the paper could still be heard in fits and starts. "And, plus five, plus seven . . . cast out the nines, zero . . ." until finally his eyes would give out and, very late, wrapped in a blanket, he would drop to the table, sobbing, "I can't go on anymore! I can't! I had such beautiful penmanship . . . !"

*   *   *   *   *

Sometimes, misfortune itself holds traces of sunshine. There had been some relief. He had been given bookkeeping jobs, but his eyesight was getting bad and living by odd jobs had become precarious. People thought him ridiculous, no one took him seriously, this fat, blubbering man who carried the weight of his daughter's fate on his shoulders. Behind his wife's back, he had mortgaged their house, and he spent his nights on his bookkeeping.

They almost always talked about their daughter as they lay in bed.

"She means everything to us."

"She's the light of our lives."

"She's so good, such a good daughter . . . !"

The old woman worked, always thinking up incoherent plans to make them rich; their clothing was spared and mended until threadbare. Everything was sparkling and they barely ate in order to save. Especially she went without, for Gebo and the girl.

"So, husband, what can you tell me? Everyone else figures things out and you're always stumped!"

"Let it be, woman! You don't understand."

"Oh, come now! Come now . . . !" And so finally, she was the one to shove him around, that fat useless man. It did him good.

"I keep struggling for the two of you," he would always say.

Every once in a while, a distant relative, Aunt Aninhas, would come to visit, and the two women would set to talking about people they knew. Some people only come around when there's trouble in the household. She was an old woman, wearing a plain black shawl, who survived on leftover misery. She always brought news—and how happy it made Gebo's wife to hear from her that people they both knew were also miserable! She felt so sorry for those that suffered as she did.

"Oh, Aninhas, I heard Desideria's in a bad way, poor thing . . . ! She's hocked everything, dear. She's starving."

And Gebo's wife, earnestly, "Starving! She's starving? Poor thing!"

"Yes, dear, it's real hunger."

"What else?"

"That's it, that's all I have to tell you. How about you? How is everything with you?"

"Now, everything's fine, thank God, we're getting by. Things are falling into place."

Meanwhile, Gebo would go to a familiar shop to meet the gathered bankrupt merchants, discipleless professors, and desperate bourgeois who'd lost everything. They would talk at length in an attempt to fool themselves. They would spur each other on, not for the sake of lying, but to bring out their yearnings, to reveal their hidden dreams. They would talk over imaginary enterprises, impossible business deals.

"Ah, I'm so happy . . . !" Gebo would say. "Now, I've got it all figured out."

They would not even listen to him and, if one of them left, the others would say, "I think he's even worse off."

"A man that used to have such good credit!"

"Now, hunger's knocking at his door."

"Poor fellow! As for me, I've gotten my hands on a sweet deal . . ."

Why aren't they working? Because bankruptcy, anguish, and ruin have thwarted their entire lives. Their energy is sapped; all they can do is dream of becoming rich. They live in an illusory world and when they lie down in their graves, they are spent, still believing in fabulous profit. And mightn't they be right after all? Won't they soon partake in that great, mysterious undertaking—Death?

VI
GABIRU'S PHILOSOPHY[1]

AND DO YOU believe in the immortality of the soul? Really believe, deep down inside?

Sometimes I believe: it's a hope, a ray of light seeping into an empty tomb through a crack between the stones. Why believe? Why not believe? Theories, words . . . Still, I'm really a materialist, just like everyone else. To sleep deep inside the rich earth is good—to sleep forever. To become a tree, light, debris, to flow through the veins of the earth, it is almost consoling—a fine dreamless sleep after the exhausting tasks of the day.

In Spring, I'm almost always materialist, in Winter, idealist, and both with equal, near ferocious sincerity.

* * * * *

To be alone, with no friends, no pressing of palms, no acquaintances, just to be free, what a dream!

To be alone out of pure cowardice, to ward off the prod of vanity's spur: "So, you don't achieve anything, but this one or that one or the devil has, they've done it!" To be alone, to dream, and to see this unique spectacle—nature; to spend my

[1] These pieces are torn from Gabiru's philosophical reflections, which he called "The Tree." Why "The Tree"? Because it was from the Tree that great branches grew and bloomed, as did deep underground roots. "The Tree" sustained itself on misery. Its roots fed on this humus—the life of the poor, of the prostitutes, of the beggars. We leave you here with parts of the book, just enough to witness Gabiru's transformation, through his contact with these humble beings and with pain, and with the promise to publish it later on, along with its conclusion.

days observing the transformations of one of those trees I can
see from here . . . !

When I shut myself away and I am alone, I am so different . . . A man is unknown even to himself, because time goes
by, death arrives, and he has never spent any time alone! If I am
by myself, voices speak to me; voices—my own, but with such
unusual words. All the beings of which I am composed babble
initially, but as I grow used to my solitude, after a while, they
speak! They preach!

*   *   *   *   *

I am convinced I was once a tree, this is why I love them so.

*   *   *   *   *

There are books that speak quietly, and books that speak loudly.
Some are enchanting, and others, strengthening. Sometimes
murmured words make more of an impression: even with the
passing of time, they awaken sleeping fibers inside us.

Why is it that water, even the humblest of puddles, is so
attractive, stimulating the dreams of men of imagination?

*   *   *   *   *

The more I despise men, the more I love nature. It is immutable.

*   *   *   *   *

Men are caught up in so much uselessness: wealth, ambition,
trivialities—they live trapped in a web. So they have no time
to see, or to listen, or to even know themselves. How many
creatures exist that have never gazed up toward the sky? Nature,
trees, mountains, rivers—this abyss I see from my room leaves
them indifferent; hours spent lazily dreaming mean nothing to

them. They have never had time to love the simple and great things in life. They have not lived the eternal. As for me, I want to eat my bread and think, let my ideas flow like a creek—as long as there is water. Some people die without ever having known they exist.

That is why I always eliminate everything that doesn't allow me to dream—and why, when I find some reason to end a friendship, I sigh with relief. One less thing to tie me down.

*   *   *   *   *

To grow accustomed to living with simple ideas is like growing accustomed to wearing old, worn-out suits. It offends people. So a person must live in isolation.

*   *   *   *   *

Death doesn't frighten me. Why? Because I only think of death as a faraway debt, still off in the distant future.

Sometimes though, at night, all of a sudden for no rhyme or reason, the idea takes hold of me quickly and shakes me down to my most hidden fibers. Then I suffocate in fear.

*   *   *   *   *

With what ease we kill even those we hold most dear . . . ! How often have I caught myself killing someone, or wishing for their death—it amounts to the same, with one addition, cowardice—people who have suffered on my behalf! For the slightest reason, the smallest of conflicts, my first thought is:

"And what if he were to die . . . ?"

Of course you will protest at once. Your heart, your background, your customs, and even your hypocrisy will protest. But, if you allow your imagination to run entirely free, it will carry out great sacrifices—for naught.

VII
SPRING

GABIRU FELT WARM, like the earth does with the onset of Spring. Ah, to create! To create . . . ! The earth, plowed and tilled by dreams alone, now traversed by this murky vein, rummaging and transforming everything—Life. The dream had consumed him, rendering him stooped and spent, lean, his eyes lost in thought.

He had finally awakened to reality and, having spent his life far away from earth and its mire, stirring the embers of his ideas, he fell in love with Mouca, who was as flat as a board. Everyone laughed at her, scrawny and pallid, with a patch on one eye, as if wearing a mask on the verge of an anguished cry.

His ideal had held his gaze like a flame, so when he lifted his eyes and came face to face with life, he'd asked: What is this . . . the world, a storm, everything I see here from my cubicle, gasping in the sunlight, penetrated with noise and shadows? Trees waving their arms at me, water, voices saturating the drenched earth? This . . . ? Is everything light, is it a flame? How beautiful it all is!

To this lean philosopher, accustomed to living with his big old tomes, seeing trees and mountains so nearby seemed as amazing as reaching the stars. Old books reveal everything except life. That's why, when he would wake up, amazed, he'd ask the brilliant waves, the rushing rivers, the extraordinary ocean, "What do you want from me?" And from way above in his garret window he would smile down at the earth, big-nosed and sad, and as somber as a funeral.

"Why do you love her, Philosopher?"

"I don't know! I love her. I feel like crying when I lay eyes on her. I love her sad eyes, her look, like a beaten dog. I love her because any other woman would ridicule an old dreamer like me. She's like I am, maybe she feels sorry for me."

We're all builders. We roam the world molding statues from the earth and our emotions. From reality and dreams we design the figures that blend into our life. Their existence is due more to what we give them of ourselves than to what they really are. From his longing, and dreams, and mire, and pity he had created an offended, sad figure, wandering and stumbling through the world, with no bread and no shelter. For him, who had spent his whole life stirring his embers, it was lucky to find Mouca, scorned by thieves and soldiers.

The women's house is dreary during the day, but at night, by the light of the oil lamp, whose fluttering renders everything speckled in a glaze of grief—broken lamps, smoky lights—it is like a circus of failures where tragic clowns make people laugh, and where thieves and chalk-faced women dramatically play out vice and crime, blending laughter and tears to make the paying audience chuckle. An Old Man arrives, who, without saying a word, laughs all night long at their being abused, and at the Dead Man, pale and sullen, with a blotch on his face. He has bony, enormous hands that are always cold and the women fear him for his cruelty, and his tragic smile.

Each one of them removes their mask and is transformed into a naked being: their features harden; their laughter, atrocious. The man wants to hear screaming. He pays and abuses. She's mire, there is no reason for pity. And the women are always singing the same sad tune, whiningly . . . Nary a one talks about her past, in fear of scorn, but they hold it inside, never forgetting. It is always the same story, eternal humus kneaded with tears. They know they were born to suffer and are resigned to it: dregs are necessary. Everything in life feeds on screams, just like the roots deep inside the earth sustain themselves with water. They are deceived and never complain. It is Fate. They do not hate those

who have led them astray, nor do they ever forget the trampled
thread of dreams they still sense in life, so far away and sad,
almost entirely dissipated. Fate gave birth to them and engulfs
them. Life is always sad—tears, beatings, and bread; such is their
fate, all the way to the grave. Listen: these wounded saplings will
someday yield a mysterious Tree.

They are sisters united, sustaining themselves on misfortune.
Their lovers grind them down and they humiliate themselves;
it is so sad not to have anyone to love. And the wretches merge
with the mud until they are finally invisible, having sacrificed
everything for the men. Miserable creatures, paid off with
insults, the lower they sink, the poorer they become, and the
closer they get to the infirmary and to death. And the smaller
they make themselves, in order to be loved. They go for days
without bread, so their lovers will have some. They will give away
their very last blouse, so they can feed their men. The whores
kill themselves if anyone disappoints them. People who live in
disgrace have learned to love only in theory. That is what love
means to grass, frogs, springs, everything in nature that is small
or deformed. For dregs, Dreams are the sole form of reality.

*   *   *   *   *

The house is tragic, with black tiles, gutters, and hallways where
all night long an oil lamp struggles.

There are consumptive women, coughing and flat chested;
there are women who insult the customers to get themselves
beaten. Gebo's daughter Sofia is tall, stooped, and so resigned
she seems dead; another girl, Luísa, whom they call Asilada,
barely speaks. She looks out sullenly, her black hair violently
loose and her face stony with sorrow.

The back of the house, filled with cubicles, is divided by a
hall. Sometimes, late at night when all is quiet, from the darkness you can hear the sound of muffled sobs.

Outside you can see the Hospital and the dark street, where

the endless human deluge carries waste, tears, and dreams. People wait, motionless on street corners . . . they seem like dark shreds, detached from night itself. They find niches under the arcades and wrap themselves in ragged scraps, torn from the blanket of darkness. Sometimes a profile emerges, with grasping hands, but everything immediately disappears underneath clothing, clothing tragically petrified like statues. Only one amputated hand is lit by the street lamp. Then sometimes the entire dull, dented figure emerges, to be immediately destroyed. The mud serves as its pedestal, the deluge passes, and the women stay there motionless, stony: if they cry, they are Pain. Some of them, from their flaming past, seem withered, others try to wane, to eclipse themselves . . . to take up no space on this earth. Nonetheless, the women go on singing the same catastrophic tune, which the night swallows up, like the tatters of trampled dreams.

*   *   *   *   *

Every night Gabiru goes off to brood in a corner. He watches Mouca wordlessly and dreams. He is known to thieves and soldiers and, seeing him enter scruffy and sad, the women exclaim, "Here comes the curse!"

And Mouca, laughingly, "The curse is here!"

But it is to no avail! With his enormous bent legs, huge hook nose, lost in thought, seeing and hearing nothing, he ponders an ideal love and talks to himself quietly, among the women, the thieves, and the soldiers:

"How I dream! I'm so shy, I set to talking and brooding . . . I brood so much . . . I get everything mixed up. How is it that you like me, when I can't even make you smile? I've been coming up with a new language, a language like that of the springs, that of the trees at the onset of March, to tell you how I feel. All words seem worn and withered. Look here, tell me something, your name is Maria, right?"

Meanwhile, the thieves and women chatter, "Can't you shut up, you bastard?"

And a scrawny, consumptive woman, all skin and bones, explains, "A fallen woman . . . What do you all have to say about fallen women? I'd just like to see you someday . . . When you don't have one scrap of bread and no one to give you any?"

And the thief answers, "You will."

"The bread I earn with my own body, who will I share it with?"

"With me."

But another woman yells from the distance, "We're just like dogs. That's right, girls, laugh! If a mother only knew to what end her daughter was raised and nurtured at her breast!" And turning to a new arrival, "Hey you, you loser, you left me black and blue the other day . . . You think a person's made of steel?"

"Get your paws off me!"

A woman asks a bald old thief, sitting off in the corner by himself, laughing in the shadows, his deformed mouth wide open, "What did you use to do, old man?"

But he keeps laughing, his huge open mouth emerges from the darkness—just like a wolf's toothless snout—and another man answers, "The old man was a worker. Just look at his hands. He smells of dirt and poverty."

The philosopher, brooding off in the corner, was watching Mouca having a good time talking with some soldiers, "I have so much to tell you—so much! And I don't know what I should say.

"If they ask me, 'What's wrong with you?' it seems as if they had woken me up and brought me back to earth.

"Trees take all Winter long to swell up with dreams and one day they wake up dreamily, destroyed. That's what happens to them.

"Just watch, March is on its way, new springs are already flowing . . . Maria is such a beautiful name!"

They talk in groups, in a hum. They are all poorly dressed, and cold. One of the women is wearing yellow socks and another one, coughing in fits, is wearing a silk shawl that does not keep her warm, "And, what did you use to do?"

"Me, nothing. Enough chatter. Kiss me?"

"Get away! Kiss you . . . ? I'd rather die. Even if I were dead I wouldn't let you kiss me. With that mug? Look at him girls . . . Have you ever seen anyone laugh like that?"

"Oh . . . you whore!" and he kicks her.

Meanwhile, off in the distance, two women are chatting in the dark.

"That day, I'll get so drunk it'll give them something to talk about."

"You?"

"Yeah."

"My mother was my cloak, she kept me warm. She was my solace, she took care of me."

And no one pays any attention to Gabiru, who is there weaving, weaving his web, all emotions and clouds, shrunken over in a corner, absorbed, neither seeing nor hearing.

"I don't really know what I feel, I've never been like this. A spout flows from my heart and waters the driest of things. I hear! What I hear . . . ! In the moonlight above, I hear mountains conversing, and trees and stones talking."

And the consumptive woman, turning to the thief, "What more do you want from me?"

And he answers, laughing, "Money, of course . . ."

"I don't even have enough left for bread, much less . . . ! I'm not fooling anyone anymore. Who would ever want me, if everyone says I'm consumptive? I'll be . . ."

"You always find some."

"Where? My clothes are all pawned, someone lent me this shawl out of charity. The scarf I was wearing yesterday? I sold it to pay my madam. And tomorrow I'm going to the hospital."

He stands up slowly to leave. Almost at the door, he murmurs, "Well, I certainly know where to get it."

Scrawny and coughing in fits, the consumptive woman

exclaims, "So go! Go ahead, if they give you more . . . ! Leave me alone!"

"I will . . ."

And she, immediately regretful, "Wait. I've given you everything. Listen . . . What have you been to me? Like a son . . ." And, turning to the other women, with a bitter smile, "Hey, girls, which one of you'll lend me some money, a little charity?"

One of them bends down. Between her sock and shoe she pulls out a coin and the consumptive woman, holding out her hand, says, "I don't earn anything anymore with my body." And she reaches out for the money and kisses it.

"Take it."

She hands it over, whispering, "Before I die, promise me you'll come see me at the Hospital? Everyone says I have TB. It's okay, but it'll be hard to die without anyone at my side . . . Who would I see? And watch your behavior when you're on your own, d'you hear me? You'll all end up behind bars, mark my words. And, if you all end up free, farewell dear friend . . . ! I'm going into the Hospital tomorrow morning, and Thursday's visiting. Don't you forget me, d'you hear? You get attached to someone and it's hard. Now what! What in the world am I supposed to do?

"A minute ago you said you knew exactly where to get some money. At Fatty's, right? Go ahead, admit it, 'cause I know anyway. I'm ready! I'm just trash, just getting in the way . . . But mind you, I've always been your friend. Just let me finish, so you won't give her that pleasure . . . I just have one thing to ask of you. You come see me before I go to my grave. To the dirt! So we just die, it's that simple. Seems so strange to me . . . What could there be in the next world? I'm ready. The doctor said so yesterday, 'You're ready!' And that's how they toss us into the cemetery . . . ! I'm still waiting for someone to tell me what we came here for . . ."

"I don't know!"

"To cry—can't think of anything else. And to lead a cursed

life." And, taking him by the hands, shyly, "So, don't forget me."

"Now, now . . . !"

And, smiling sadly, piously, her pale lips lighting up like a ray of sunshine, "'Now, now', that's all you men know how to say. You men are all the same, you talk out of the same mouth. Poor us! We get attached, then death comes along and takes everything with it."

Gabiru uncrosses his legs and stands up, murmuring to himself, "What times we live in. As if it's made up of emotions . . . And everything keeps dreaming its own dream, that much I know, I know I feel it in the trees, the stones, and the earth, even in the parched earth . . . And there's so much I wanted to tell you! So much . . . ! Listen, are you still called Maria?"

VIII
LUÍSA'S MEMORIES

THIS IS HOW one of the women's stories goes:

I've always been cold. Feeling like my bones are cold goes way back to when I was little.

      *   *   *   *   *

I never had a mother, I had no one. I shut my eyes now and all I see is the Orphanage, the damp hallways, the dormitory, and the cold, vaulted refectory ceiling covered in granite. All that stone seemed like a tomb, like we were buried.

      *   *   *   *   *

There's something else I remember from when I was little: I always wanted someone to kiss, and never had anyone. Everyone I knew was rough with me.

Let me try to remember . . . First it's all confusing, then the mist breaks up and I remember my sad life at the Orphanage.

We'd get up to pray when it was still dark out. A bell would ring. We could barely walk, we'd stumble like old women. Some of the girls needed help getting dressed. The Sister would yell if we took too long. They'd pull us out of that morning drowsiness as if they were dragging us from our graves and oblivion. We'd have been better off if they'd have let us sleep forever. Why did we come into this world?

*   *   *   *   *

Out of all the girls I knew, almost all of them, luckily, died 'cause
they had no mother.

*   *   *   *   *

All of them, even when they were still so little, seemed like they
were already grown up. And they had a way about them, bitter,
grave, and suffering, like they'd had a hard life. They'd play off
in the corner, never laughing, with toy animals and little stones.
Once, one of them said out loud, "Oh, mommy . . . !"

And it was a scandal. Where had the girl, who had no mother,
learned to pronounce that word?

*   *   *   *   *

Can you believe it? In my only image of them they seem old
and withdrawn, like sad old women with no children.

*   *   *   *   *

Even so, I like longing for that dark life at the Orphanage.

*   *   *   *   *

There were cows in a corral that gave us watery milk. Once,
when I was already big, one cow was always moaning. I felt so
sorry I asked the gardener what was wrong with her.

"She's sad because they took her baby from her."

And to think some mothers toss their babies out!

Must be terrible for a mother to die, leaving a child to the
Orphanage!

There were big girls, and medium and small. The big girls

were clumsy, with enormous hands and coarse, black dresses. All of them were ugly.

There was some kind of grace missing that you only see in girls with mothers, no matter how ugly they are: abandoned creatures, sickly plants . . .

*   *   *   *   *

Sometimes the director of the board would visit us. He was a harsh man, severe and clean-shaven, and he'd come to remind us that we lived off charity.

"You must always remember this: you owe your lives to your benefactors."

He himself was one. His picture was up on the wall with all the others, in the same funereal frame. It was the last one in the enormous, freezing, echo-filled room, filled with pictures all over the place. The benefactors!—More like a gallery of drowned people, all solemn, dry, mean, severe, and thin-lipped, with serious expressions.

Every night the Sisters made us pray for them, to whom we owed our daily bread.

*   *   *   *   *

It was forbidden to talk, except during recess, and that might explain the lines we all had at the sides of our mouths, even the youngest.

*   *   *   *   *

The best place in the Orphanage was the infirmary because it was the warmest, the sun came in all day long, and you could see the trees on the property. And also because the Sister-nurse was the only one who kissed us and had a heart. We were all her friends.

It's strange. I remember the big trees you could see from there, but I only remember them scrawny and naked, against a pale sky.

* * * * *

It seems like my knees are still cold and painful. I haven't been able to warm them since.

* * * * *

The bread at the Orphanage tasted like no other bread I've ever eaten, no matter how bad off I ever was: a bitter, reheated flavor. The whole cafeteria had the same smell. Everything, even the crucifix, even the watery broth, the miserable rations they'd give us, all seemed to say to us, "Listen, remember you live off charity! Get used to misery!"

* * * * *

Can you believe it? It'd be much more charitable just to drown motherless children. You'd be saving them from the Orphanage, from charity, from life.

* * * * *

Everything in the dormitory was basic, bleached, and monotonous and, although white, funereal. The sun, which came in through little windows opening out of a prison wall, was pale and, even in summer, seemed like a winter sun; the beds, all white, were lined up against the washed, naked walls; only at the very back, above the Sister's bed, was there a blue china Christ, a stain on all that whiteness.

We didn't have recess in the convent yards. We used to play silently inside the cloister. It seemed as if they were afraid of showing us the trees and shadows. The cloister . . . Up above you could always see, set inside the eaves, a rectangle of sky, and the geometric shadow stretched all the way down. One side was always cold and damp: there was moss on the walls. In the middle of the cloister a little stone dolphin spouted a trickle of freezing water, drop by drop, through its decaying teeth. The whole place had the frightening, damp serenity of a tomb. Only the swallows cut through the sky above; but once when they came in March, exhausted and chirping, to make their nests in the beams, the nuns beat them down. Why destroy them? Their remains stayed around the cloister for a long time, scraps of warm down, tender you could say. They would get handed around excitedly. Some of the orphans stared at them curiously; the youngest girls would play with them.

One of them said, "It's a cradle . . ."

*   *   *   *   *

Why destroy them? So we wouldn't find out that birds have mothers that take care of their children? So we wouldn't miss our own, whom we'd never known? So we wouldn't know all that . . . ? But how naive of the Sisters if that was their reasoning! We suspected, we guessed it all. And when one of the littlest girls explained to the others playing ring-around-the-rosy, "It's the birdies' crib . . ."—how many of us had already thought of a crib like that, all warm and soft!

*   *   *   *   *

There would then come a day when we were taken from that monotonous, harsh life, when we were big girls and the director came to drag us off.

It was a solemn day. We were to leave. Whoever needed a maid that didn't eat much could find one at the Orphanage. A notebook, papers, a few rags, ill-fitting blouses, and the director's speech:

"This Orphanage has supported you out of charity. If you're alive today, it is because of your benefactors. So you be sure to always remember what they did for you in your prayers. And be thankful to those that take you in. They take you in out of the goodness of their hearts."

And so, grasping our bundle, we went out to face Life.

*   *   *   *   *

Oh! My dear mother!

IX
GABIRU'S PHILOSOPHY

To HAVE THE same right to immortality as do the trees and the animals humbles me, and by making me humble, I become better, more of a brother to the small and miserable.

*   *   *   *   *

Only suffering creatures are worthy of life, and in reality they are the only ones that live.

*   *   *   *   *

In infinite time and limited space, molecules form groups and split apart . . . Only chemistry, only chemistry exists . . . Molecules, which are made up of the life force, are one day trees, and the next, animals, stones, and men. According to what? What shapes them?

This is me: I have existed, and always will, as a being in this tragic ocean, whatever chance determines, according to my molecules, split apart tomorrow, joining others later on . . . Thus I've lived up until now—and so will continue throughout eternity.

So, now that it's my turn to be a man, I must live so, drawing from my own existence: the *universe* inside me, my former self, should speak—the stones and the trees—the humble beast.

Your opinion . . . ? What good does it do me? And is it yours, do you feel it is really yours, or is it learned, false, from other men that want to stifle me?

What should my goal be? To allow my whole universe to speak, allow all that is inside me to preach in its hoarse voice— in its own voice and not in yours. If I have hatred, let me be Hatred; if I have laughter, let me be Laughter.

This is a unique moment, it must not be missed. Through which chance? Through which insane fury, after which rebellions, after how many hours or centuries of goading, of despair and rage, will these molecules, lost in an ocean larger than the Atlantic, once again exist, join together to gain awareness of the Universe? And now you come, you, man, and want to silence them with your laws, your theories, your dreams . . .

It is a unique moment: lost tomorrow. Centuries of toil to gain awareness of the universe, in just one minute; centuries of dreams flickering in the depth of obscurity, and still, to see no light; centuries of bitterness, of struggle, of aborted attempts— and still, to be unable to live. It is like reaching a tree and tearing away its foliage.

But look: everything around you is content, because it is all fulfilling its destiny. You fulfill yours. Everything is harmonious, because it is leading its true life: plants grow free of others' imposition of rules, the animals, all of nature has neither regrets nor doubts. Nor will you, if you live your true life and not someone else's.

This should be your education: make the universe you carry within you speak, with its own voice. Rid yourself, kill, and trample anything that thwarts you in this endeavor. Do you know how many centuries it will take to once again gain this awareness? And how many lost efforts, how many battles it will take? How much crying out?

*   *   *   *   *

Revel in everything: misfortune, hunger, the earth, the sun, laughter, everything, because it will be beyond endless centuries before you ever feel them again. Soak up life, take up a large share of life, so when you reach the gates of Nothing you can say: "I lived!"

*   *   *   *   *

Your obligations to yourself come first, before your obligations to others.

*   *   *   *   *

You should love rivers, because you were once a river; mountains, because you once roamed their depths; the clouds, your sisters; the trees in whose sap you have swum—and man, because you are a man.

*   *   *   *   *

If they do not allow you to be what you should be—resist.
It is better to die than to not put up a fight. In death you will triumph because you will have fulfilled your destiny.

*   *   *   *   *

You are made of humus, you are made of earth, and if the earth gave you a mouth, why? So that you would speak. To what end did it create so many mouths? So that after thousands of attempts, words that must be spoken, are spoken . . . On that day everything will have a voice. In fact there will not be one spring, one tree, one beast, no matter how forgotten, one stone, no matter how ignored, that does not have a voice and that does not make its confession.

*   *   *   *   *

Modern education, on the contrary, tends toward this end: that everyone in the universe speak in exactly the same manner.

*   *   *   *   *

Our destiny is born along with us. Not to fulfill it, no matter what it is, is to be miserable.

*   *   *   *   *

Each creature, born yesterday, takes how many centuries to come into being? Do you know . . . ?

*   *   *   *   *

Do not go against life. We are a deluge that God created for a reason . . . And thus, there will be born those who incarnate Evil, you'll say . . . Because evil too has a mouth, a mouth that speaks with no stammer.

*   *   *   *   *

If nature creates monsters, it is because they are necessary, like a cleansing abscess.

*   *   *   *   *

When all is said and done, the tigers never get away.

*   *   *   *   *

And what's the use of pretense?

*   *   *   *   *

Inside him, man has particles of everything that exists in the universe: metals, stones, etcetera. It is a compact universe. Depending on which molecules predominate, he either hates or loves.

When will chemistry become so great as to be able to make this analysis?

*   *   *   *   *

There are people who have never done us any harm, and yet we despise them. Never? Who knows . . . ? If you live an eternity, if you have always existed and are eternal?

*   *   *   *   *

What makes up sincere, overwhelming inner piety? Memories.

*   *   *   *   *

Let us flee the earth, they say. No, stay close, the refined earth that is you, the earth that is your mother. The essence of the earth, the frenzied work of her womb over the course of centuries upon centuries, you must not renounce her! Love her, love life. You may be the earth's dream. She has put inside you all of her emotion, all of her maternity, all of her pain, and also all of her that is immaterial: she gave you your dream. Be good, according to her orders; bad, according to her will.

*   *   *   *   *

Some days a person feels responsible for all the evil wielded in this world.

*   *   *   *   *

Throughout the world huge rivers of molecules flow and repel—
rivers of hatred, rivers of love and of bitterness, laughter, and
dreams . . .

X
GEBO'S STORY

THERE HE GOES, stumbling, rumpled, and ridiculous.

Pain too makes him ludicrous and the tears on his big surprised face just make us laugh. Life pushes him along, throws him, knocks him down on the street, nervous, without a helping hand—and with his disheveled white hair.

People call out, "Hey Gebo! Hey Gebo . . . !"

You do not have to take pity on the weak. Nature herself repels them from her breast.

*   *   *   *   *

The cupboards were bare, everything in the house was in shreds. They slept in cots on the floor, on those cold Winter nights. It was hardest for him to watch his daughter mulling for hours on end. Over what . . . ? When Gebo thought about Sofia's hard luck, it wrenched his heart. She was the only reason he still fought destiny. And there was barely enough bread to feed her!

And his wife would cry out, "But work! You don't work . . . ! You're just a big ne'er-do-well. Look how everyone else plods along, how they get ahead . . . You're an idiot! In this world, you've got to have a lot of savvy. People like you shouldn't marry!"

"Oh, woman, once you're down, you can't get back on your feet."

And eventually, he had been knocked down for the last time, he had no more energy, no more strength, he was prostrate. He wanted to lie down and never wake up again. He had been everywhere, knocked on every door, had humiliated himself, and had begged; only to be treated badly, hear cruel words, and be sent on his way. His friends, who in the beginning would give him handouts just to belittle him, now spoke harshly, "Come back later! It's too much! You can't go on like this forever, you're taking advantage."

His best hours were spent sleeping, deeply, a well he would dive into as soon as he fell asleep. That part of his life, hidden from misery, without thought, without dreams, only a profound sense of annihilation, was Gebo's only pleasure. And the more misfortune defeated him, the more caring he was, and the deeper he slept. In contrast to his wife, who barely slept and spent the entire night fretting and crying, as soon as he fell into bed he dropped off like a corpse. Sometimes his wife would not even let him rest; she wanted to talk, to discuss, to hear him . . .

"You're sleeping like a hog! Say something, listen to me!"

And Gebo, his lids drooping, would start trying to form a few words, incoherently, until she would exclaim furiously, "Go to sleep! Move over!"

But he had to wake up and face the obligatory daily search for some measly spare change, a search by then crazed and cruel. People could see him dashing, spying out a long lost friend, tracking him down, telling him his trials in a broken voice, then in a quiet murmur, pleading. He would loiter for hours outside a shop, this doddering old man, in his threadbare coat, mended by his daughter, waiting and hoping some acquaintance would go by. Sometimes the days would disappear and he still had no money for bread—because hearts are made of stone. He would circle the streets in despair. Could he not find one person to help him out? They would cast him aside, and he would make himself humble, without bitterness, scrounging and always sweating. He had nothing more to hock and thought often about death.

His heart heavy, he would once again spy out his friends, in endless despair. As soon as he got home, choking and gloomy, his wife awaiting him in a trance would ask, "So, what? What?"

"Here it is, woman! Here it is!"

Oh . . . to rest, to sleep in the heavy, deep earth, to escape the exhausting tears forever, to forget the humiliations, the bitter hours chasing after people he had once helped! To remain in the final sleep, to never awake again, neither to misfortune nor to scorn!

What had he ever done to God and to everyone else to deserve such relentless punishment, suffering hunger, and cold, and the disgrace of his daughter? There was no rest for him, not even in his own home. The nagging and yelling were endless. Only Sofia, beautiful and sad in her resignation, lifted his spirits. If it were not for her, how good it would be simply to die . . . ! His friends were rich and as harsh as stones. Some of them looked right through him: others laughed and would give him nothing. And thus deeper and deeper, stuck in his misfortune, fat and ludicrous, dazed and begging, with a single idea upon awakening daily: to manage to find some measly spare change so the women could eat.

Shabby and spent, every single day they repeated the exact same words, experienced the same distress. Damp, terrified, and cold—real cold, the kind only misery brings on—huddled together, every once in a great while they were warmed by some vain dream. They stared blankly, lost, absorbed by reality, and their surrounding Misfortune seemed to be laughing. They wore out their last clothes, by then they did not even have any used clothing . . . And he was increasingly fat and increasingly flaccid. If, perchance, they were to laugh over some trifle, the three of them together, that laughter caused even more distress than their very tears. Many a night they did not light the lantern and the three of them ended up sleeping on the same cot.

Their little house and garden, passed down through the generations, was the last thing sold, and was worth the remaining tears in their smarting eyes. They had to accept losing the trees they had planted with their own hands, the vegetable garden, the stream, and the old fruit trees, loved as if they were people.

Yet, they still carried it all, as part of their being, as a reminder of their happier days, the sun that still provided warmth, and that would never sparkle again.

His wife no longer nagged: she had succumbed with a confused gaze, and now spent her days in incoherent monologues. And he stayed there, fat and ridiculous, battered from all the jostling.

"Hey Gebo!"

"Huh? Huh . . . ?"

XI
LUÍSA AND THE DEAD MAN

THE THIEF WAS hiding. They were pursuing him, he had fled, gotten away. That night, with a crust of bread stored under his worn shirt, he found himself at the harbor. The sky was dark and the murky river flowed like lava. Water is frightening at night: it talks, entices, and its chill is reminiscent of a grave. The water's noises sound like a choir of murmuring, foreboding voices.

It was a quiet night, humid and stifling. The surroundings were dimly lit, the water was splashing up against the rocks, flowing into the old harbor piles. And the only other sound came from the bleak night, choked, rushed, breathing, human—tragic lapping from the depths of the silent, opaque night.

The Dead Man held the bread closer to his chest—his dinner—and sighed with relief. No one would look for him there, it was as if he were buried at the bottom of the river. He had not eaten for two days and was finally about to take his first bite. His knees hurt and he felt enormously weary. As he sat down, he bumped into a body, fallen and abandoned. He jumped up, startled, holding the bread he was about to bite into, "Who's there?"

No one: only the dark night and the sound of the river pounding up against the rocks.

"Oh!"

As he felt around he found a motionless girl. Her skirt was soaking wet and her feet were cold.

"She must be dead." And relieved, he sat down to eat his bread. But he sensed her moving. "Another miserable person . . ." He wondered, "Who's there?"

And from the darkness a child's voice began speaking, "It's me."

"Who are you?"

"No one."

"What are you doing here?"

"I'm not doing anything."

"Then what do you want?"

"I came to jump into the river."

"Ah . . . !"

"But I was scared. The river water is always colder than death."

The dense night and the relentless preaching sound of the water. The low clouds surrounded them in dark fluid and they were both swallowed up by the deserted night. They could not see each other and those two voices, one of them quiet and childish, and the other hoarse, were like a dialogue between two unknown forces swirled into the same infinite whirlpool by chance.

The Dead Man asked her, "What's your name?"

"Luísa."

"Who hurt you?"

"No one, I'm pregnant."

"Ah . . . !"

"I'm pregnant. I didn't know anything. I'm pregnant, it's all over. Why don't they tell us everyone's out to hurt us? A person has to learn."

"Learn what?"

"To be miserable. I haven't eaten in two days. I've been wandering around. They sent me away, they kicked me out, and I'm just wandering around, crying."

"Go home."

"I'm from the Orphanage, I don't have anyone, not even a mother, nothing."

"Did they do you wrong?"

"No, no one did anything. I didn't understand. When I left the Orphanage, I didn't know anything. Then one day I turned up pregnant and they sent me away. No one'll have anything to do with me in this condition. When a girl's in the family way, there's nothing can be done. It's not our fault . . ."

"Didn't you make the baby?"

"I was innocent."

"Ah . . . !"

"I didn't know anything, cross my heart."

"So what happened?"

"I got put out of the Orphanage and I went into service. My master's the one who did this."

It's always the same old situation, tragic. A man finds a poor, defenseless, helpless creature, leads her on and exploits her. She left the Orphanage with nothing but her bundle in her arms and the Director of the Board's farewell speech, and went into service. No sooner did the master lay his eyes on that girl with nary a soul to look out for her, than he drew her aside in whispers.

"It was like they tore my heart out . . ."

She listened. Then with a sad smile, revealing the sharp teeth of hunger, she stayed there pensive, talking to herself for hours. Her poor, starved, abandoned body, with the lingering odor of the infirmary, the body that had already come into this world with this sad destiny—to be exploited. The master soon lost interest, and she stayed there, serving them with the same smile, but paler and sad. One day she woke up pregnant and the mistress put her out on the street. She rummaged through Luísa's belongings and screamed, "I should call the police."

With a child in her womb and her bundle in her arms she started going from door to door, but was sent away as soon as they saw her belly, until she finally ended up at the river, hungry and stiff with cold.

She stopped talking. All that could be heard was the lapping of the tide. And the preaching of the river. You, river, what do you carry in your waters that keeps you talking all night long? You carry tears with you, and roots, and bodies: you have soaked the earth, ground bread, and moistened tree trunks. And between the willows, mirroring the silver moon, you have been romantic and sad. Then you bathed the city stones; its iron and your voice became foreboding. You carry salty tears to their destiny; you carry everything, sighs, confessions, remains out to the ocean deep. What do you have to say, river? What do you preach? Do you tell of your incessant life? To go out to the wide open sea, into deep eddies, to then travel like clouds, sometimes dark, sometimes golden at sunset, traversed by the sun, warmed and enlivened, to finally fall in rain, to quench the earth's thirst, and to return to the bosom of the planet; and then, to finally burst out again in springs, carrying different tears, different dreams and roots in the same eternal condemnation, laboring furiously. Is that it? Is it to grind black bread that you flow over familiar trunks, ever the river, the deep ocean, or clouds . . . ?

A little light, shining from the distance, leaving a trembling golden streak on the water, had all but disappeared, and so the Dead Man in the silent darkness spoke.

"And you, what do you think about this?"

"Think about what, sir?"

"Life. That's all anyone wants, is to take advantage. The rich abuse the poor; the poor steal from the rich. Everyone wants to make everyone else weep."

"Everyone?"

"Everyone. I myself could kill you right now, I can do you any harm I feel like. Don't scream, that only makes it worse. No one's coming to your rescue."

"I won't scream."

"Your mother sent you away so she wouldn't have to take care of you and your master took advantage of you. So, what do you think? Besides, what choice did you have but to let him? What could you do? They're always going to take advantage and you'll only never be abandoned by . . ."

"Who?" she asked anxiously.

"Hunger. You'll wander around here until you drop dead, kicked around and living in misery. Misery beats all, no one in the world is stronger. If you're hungry, they'll laugh at you for sure, and give you dirt to eat."

"But sir! Sir! Then why did they care for me at the Orphanage? They should have let me die. I never hurt anyone. What should I do? I have the shirt on my back. I pawned my skirt. I haven't eaten in two days."

"Kill yourself. Why did you come down to the river?"

"To drown myself . . . but I'm afraid of water . . . ! When I put my feet in that dark water, I ran away . . . Ah, mother, my dear mother!"

And she fell over.

The Dead Man put his hands on her. She was soaking wet, her whole poor body, still not fully grown, frozen and paralyzed.

"What's wrong with you?"

"Nothing. Just hungry."

"Here, take my bread."

And the thief gave her all the bread he had.

XII
GABIRU'S PHILOSOPHY

No MATTER WHAT, if immortality exists it must be very different from anything anyone has ever imagined.

*   *   *   *   *

To be broken, oppressed, and scorned almost always makes a man great because it shocks and awakens dormant voices.

*   *   *   *   *

I understand the sincere materialist, the sincere idealist. In the former, the earth prevails, in the latter, the clouds. Everything that is true, ingrained, and profound is beautiful—even crime.

*   *   *   *   *

It doesn't matter where the concept of immortality came from, what matters is whether or not it exists. Everyone senses it, even the most materialist, everyone knows it shines in the depths of our being. You can shake it, smother it with theories, words, and paltry explanations, but what you cannot do, is uproot it. It is like some trees that always leave their deep, imperturbable roots in the soil, even when chopped down. To kill them you would have to make the earth sterile.

Every man carries immortality within himself like a certainty or aspiration . . . It moves beneath all ashes.

But what is immortality?

*   *   *   *   *

I take everything seriously, even trifles—one more reason to be miserable.

*   *   *   *   *

And when do I fulfill my destiny?—you might say. Ask yourself.

*   *   *   *   *

If trees were not necessary, would trees still exist? If criminals were not necessary, would there, perchance, still be criminals?

*   *   *   *   *

As for our education, it is best forgotten. It should be forgotten because it has nothing to do with life, it is something else entirely. What we acquire, costing our nerves, blood, sweat, plus everything learned in battle—that's what we take to our grave. That's real education.

*   *   *   *   *

Man always seeks the philosophy most compatible with his temperament, his mistakes—even with his crimes. If it doesn't exist, he invents it.

*   *   *   *   *

I think, contrary to popular opinion, I am no man's friend, except initially. At first, rough edges aren't seen or else they're disguised. Then they start to harden.

    I believe you only have friends until you're twenty, when you still haven't thought about life. Then you get hardened. Over the course of a serious and calculated life, men rarely maintain friendships.

For us to be friends, one of us must submit to the other.

*   *   *   *   *

No, death does not destroy the essence of life, but in breaking down a form death destroys the conscience of that form, which is made up of thousands of consciences.

The actions of what we call the spirit over my matter produce my "I" with the inevitable mistakes, dreams, despair, and hatred. The same force draws distinct harmonies from a harp or from an organ. What's left, then? The essence of life?

*   *   *   *   *

The predominance of certain molecules produces a dreamer; the predominance of others, the hero, etcetera. That is the chemistry of the future.

*   *   *   *   *

It is not a question of being happy or miserable; instead, it is a question of fulfilling the destiny to which you were born.

*   *   *   *   *

What a false truth, to suppose that life has a single purpose—happiness or misery! Does that not imply subordinating the universe to mankind?

If life has a purpose—it is to live. Live, allow ourselves to fulfill the destiny to which we were born. That is logical, inevitable, more certain than we imagine, and more beautiful—but still too early to glimpse.

*   *   *   *   *

Man is a fountain where life flows crystal clear, or murky, a trickle emotion renders golden or else transforms into a choleric, black rush.

One day the fountain dries up.

*   *   *   *   *

The earth must always create its types, whether or not that pleases man. Man is nothing more than the essence of the universe and is born so that everything may have a mouth. We can attempt to restrain this with dikes, delay the deluge, but one day the wide river of Life and of Destiny will burst.

*   *   *   *   *

No, no, it's not fair that people die suddenly without protest, words, or shouts, die with their mistakes, ambitions, and dreams . . . A grave is suddenly opened . . . There is no more thought, no vision or sound . . . The pain is not from leaving loved ones, or habits—the pain is to not live. To die when life goes on in the same harmonious, impassive manner—that is the horror.

*   *   *   *   *

No man in the universe truly exists for another, he exists for no other life except his own.

*   *   *   *   *

At the age of thirty, friends are abandoned. If any remain, it's out of habit, or interest: it is calculated. If you want to continue loving others, draw away, become a hermit. Or be insincere, live a lie. The battle has begun: you must withdraw, win—and everyone at this age is what they are. There is no more molding: like steel, unsheathed, just out of the forge. They have established habits, vanities, and lies. All things previously sketched have hardened. Carved in stone.

So, if you want to live among others, you have to pretend. There are hundreds of others your age on the same path as you, and after the same ends.

Ahead of you, there are the men of forty, who must either be removed, conquered, or fooled. Each one of them is of steel. To triumph, you must flatter them, you must be them and not yourself.

Those with strong personalities withdraw because they can never please. Triumph does not belong to the strong, nor to the most intelligent, but to those who, with no personality, can be everyone.

To be similar is to flatter: that means you have to strap on a mask, just like that of men you mean to conquer.

*   *   *   *   *

Yes, life is a splendid tragedy, with all of its crimes, dreams, and hatred. Within us, the mountains, trees, and clouds speak and, in a murmur, they even speak of what is yet unknown.

What is required for each one to find himself? What is required for frail trees to sprout flowers? The Spring—and Pain.

You, Earth, are the mother; and you, Pain, have impregnated her, and the faint murmur of the earth's cries reaches us.

I love you in the animals, the sun, light, and stones; in the earth where I dig my hands until they're black, in the water that washes them, in the air I breathe, in the dream; in death, in disgrace; in all that is humble or great, it matters not.

XIII
THIS SLIP OF A GIRL

I STAY HERE thinking, so alone in this big old house . . . ! At night I hear voices, soon muffled, that want to speak to me, but cannot. Only my past crimes (long forgotten!) set to preaching inside me. The fire flickers in the dark and I sense the surrounding night entirely inhabited.

It has been twenty years, but still, during certain foreboding hours, something inside me stirs and awakens. Oh, no! I am all too familiar with the shape of connecting ideas, even the most contradictory, and with the way some trifle recalls an old, repressed crime. But that's not it: it's from the depth of my being that the images erupt, detached, meaningless, like ghosts. Sometimes when I'm alone and forgotten a rustle comes from behind, reminding me; other times I wake up suddenly in the middle of the night, already thinking about that poor, exploited little creature. Life's rumblings and other accumulated crimes can make me forget her image, but there always comes the day when I cry out, "Abandoned! Abandoned . . . !"

Yet, nevertheless, the event itself is banal, clichéd, as common as the little street urchin herself, soaked to the bones and whose name I never even discovered, because I didn't bother to ask her.

Just to be like everyone else, out of vanity I convinced her to follow me when I ran into her one afternoon, with no bread, thrown out of her house, wandering the sorrowful streets. Would she be fifteen? Yes, she told me fearfully, she was. And I, taking her to the brothel, felt neither proud nor happy, but oppressed and ashamed. I was already asking myself: how am I to get rid of her?

There was nothing more basic, nothing purer or simpler. I left her hastily, after handing over some money to the fat, cross-eyed woman, who was smiling, and then I fled, like someone fleeing remorse.

That was all. So why is it then—and it's been years—that in certain moments of silence I remember the poor creature and her innocent words, the smile of the cross-eyed woman and the poor skinny body, soaked with rain, and entirely hurt by life?

I can see her right here, barefoot in the dark, drenched to her bones and smiling at me, a pitiful, tearful smile, a smile so sad it still wrenches my heart.

The fire flickers in the darkness, entirely inhabited with voices that would preach, but are soon silenced, suffocated. There is a gust of wind outside and on the stairwell you can hear the pall-bearer's footfalls; the women chortle and I remain alone, thinking, in this big old house, my eyes glued to the dying flame . . .

There he is in the stairwell coughing, his chest raspy and hoarse.

In fact, I know of no other man as boring and banal as him. As banal as banality itself. Smiling, loving, and even with his broken heart, he was always held up to ridicule. Even his enemies pitied him or held him in disdain. Yes, pity or disdain, because Senhor José was incapable of hatred. He could never learn to avenge himself and people knew it. He even did me a good turn, which I later repaid with spare change when I ran into him, prostrate on the street one day. I never discovered even one interesting thing about him: his life is the life of every creature that sinks for a lack of any sort of practical notion of how to fight: mudslinging, lies, and then, to finally triumph. Life (ah . . . all sound philosophies teach it) belongs to the strong and able . . . But today I'm irritable and I feel alone in this big old house. It seems as if the night had voices and that my past crimes (long ago forgotten!) have finally found words and have set to speaking inside me.

It is perhaps to overcome this obsession that I set to pondering over the life of this man, who is as banal as banality itself.

I don't know how to tell the story, what words can narrate an existence that is like a discarded rag, soaked in tears.

Yes, crazy. And he was never happy. One day catastrophe came along and burned his house down: later they tricked him, lied to him. And there was no lack of illness to scar him, boring into his face, nor tuberculosis to burst his chest with coughing, nor misery to bring him down. And that is why, as he removes the casket from each house, as if tearing it from the chests of those left behind, he most certainly laughs to himself, he must be laughing, comforted.

Oh, Senhor José, who was your mother?

*   *   *   *   *

As he makes his way to the burials boys throw rocks at him, neighbors flee; Rata is the only one that speaks to the pallbearer.

Rata is his equal, just as mistreated by destiny as he is. She has always been ugly, scrawny, and sad. Her life has been nothing but work. First she supported the woman that took her in from the Orphanage, and then the man she married, who soon left her on her own. With Senhor José, she occasionally passes the time of day. They always say the same things and with the same paltry words! She barely knows how to express herself. Their talk is like stones communicating, two beings rolling along together in the same huge wave of life, by chance. They don't even complain—what is there to complain about? They are in God's fatherly hands.

"We're poor," he says.

"We're poor," she replies. "And sometimes, hungry."

"Yes, we are."

"When my dear mother was alive, I scraped by, starving. I had to support her and I barely made enough for me. Until her work was finally done. Everything ends one day or another."

"It's worse not to have anyone at all. It's worse than hunger."

"It's the worst of all."

"What's to be done?"

"Do you know what, Mister? I tell you, sometimes I just sit and think, why do we suffer so . . ."

*   *   *   *   *

The wind howls. In the heart of Winter the deluge rushes, carrying the tears that have soaked the earth; gusts drag cries off to an unknown destiny. The tears of the poor roll inside some lost cloud and the wind carries away their sighs, moans, and words. Black night! Black night! The flame flickers, as does the building, under the gusty wind.

So here I am, absorbed in the burning coals, fascinated by their crimson color, or else staring at this other flame, the Hospital, which shines in the darkness like crying embers.

You would almost say the stone from which it was built was numbed. They've kept adding on: granite upon granite as the misery has increased. They ripped it from the heart of the earth. It was once the skeleton of the mountains, where the roots clung, a hidden crag thriving on stored up water; then it sensed the water gurgle in its breast and, reaching for light, that rock, the earth's sister, buried in the earth, met with this fate—to house the wretched.

At the foot of the stone the Tree grows. It preaches the universe and is invigorated. Its roots spread out underground all the way to the Hospital and its branches nearly cover the building. On one side, the Hospital; on the other, the Tree. Only they prosper. The Tree's boughs keep spreading and each Winter the granite increases, like one more stone tree. Through one there runs sap, through the other, cries. The Hospital has roots throughout the city.

The Tree is almost a building. The trunk is corroded and the boughs up top twist and send out new growths. Its roots will eventually suck up the Hospital. Over the years, they have stuck to the granite, little by little penetrating it, making grooves to dig more deeply into the human misery.

And over there? What's over there? As the days end, I sense a lively breeze, the breath of sleeping mountains banging on the dense walls of the Hospital; and also noises, brightness, and a mixture of gold and green, the gurgling of mines, raining sunshine and water, falling. The earth gasps, the mountains swell, and through the air swirl the sighing of trees, the murmur of fountains, the breath of unknown plants. Oh, nightfall, soaked in moonlight, when you can hear the tears of still waterwheels, buckets dropping one by one onto the parched earth, and you can sense the dreamlike dialogues amongst the wild pines . . .

And the Tree, in reaction to this noise, is made dizzy, shaken to the very depth of its roots.

*   *   *   *   *

Wait! Wait . . . ! The gusty wind gets stronger. Followed by an exhausted silence, silence worse than the gales, wherein I hear the world's strained effort to cry out—filling the darkness. The darkness gasps and the last of the embers still gleam in the fireplace, whose crimson gasps and pants until finally dying out.

I cry out! It's always the same girl who emerges, thin, pale, and sad, her poor dress soaked in rain or drenched in tears. She smiles at me, barefoot, reaching out for me. It's her! It's her . . . ! There's but one live coal in the fireplace, blending dusty crimson into the darkness. And it is going out! It is dying.

All of life is built on cries, with each step forward a small creature is always squashed . . . What do you expect?

It isn't hatred she feels for me, because her smile, which I sense damp with tears, is sad, yet resigned. Nonetheless, regret awakens, regret sets to growling . . . I see the fat, cross-eyed woman give her money; I see her head out to the streets, soaked to the bones, without realizing she has been mistreated, tricked, thrown out . . . Will she scream? What is the point of crying out on the face of this earth, can you all tell me that?

Who in the world can she count on? And she doesn't understand. She walks barefoot through deserted streets, in the rain. Through this very harsh life, abandoned. Someone else comes along and tricks her, lies to her. What is the point of crying out on the face of this earth? She must suffer and resign herself to brutality, scorn, and laughter. Grow accustomed to exploitation, lies, and infamy. People laugh as she walks by, drenched in tears and drowned in misery. And thus she heads out into the world, where . . . ? To where?

Ah, those last embers, still gleaming like golden dust, those embers, dying out in the hearth, now nearly entirely black . . . ! The crazy gales are outside, crying. How many people cry out in this vale of tears! At the same time, how many are screaming, crushed, with no one willing to lend a hand? To what end are the cries, can you tell me that . . . ? That last streak of fire is like the last thread of a dying soul.

And she comes back, turns around! Her poor limp body, born to suffer, already hurt by life, dressed in a little skirt, and the resigned smile of one who already knows what awaits her— so many cries! So many tears out there!

*   *   *   *   *

The darkness has closed in. I suffocate . . . !

XIV
SCORN

IN THE DESERTED night, Gabiru is weaving his web:

Matter also dreams. In this mixture of men and boulders, this deluge carrying cries and raging forces, this tornado drawn out beyond eternity, it makes a difference whether something is born stone or cloud, born in the apple tree in a remote, humble yard or in the shimmering water rushing off a cliff. It is not by chance that molecules attract and repel to dissolve into other forms. There are bodies that chemistry is unable to link, because they are separated by hatred, and others that join together voraciously.

After death, matter goes into an ocean. Rivers carry the molecules, until they meet up with those they are meant to join. My heart joined to yours will grow into a simple thorn bush. It will be in some modest place, but any passersby this April will be forever moved. My brain will seek out yours to float together in the serenity of some river. Whether on earth or in rocks, I will look for you unconsciously till I find and enjoy you in this stormy ocean. And if you are a fountain, I'll discover you and together we will quench the thirst of many a forgotten root.

*   *   *   *   *

Simple creatures will become trees, so dwarfed we are moved at the sight of them. Dreamers, shredded into clouds, will journey salty ocean sunsets, and the clusters of rocks where the sun burns down, those eternal clusters of rocks will be made from the hearts of the wicked.

*   *   *   *   *

Just look how wonderful, this extraordinary miracle, this life that Pita has shown me: trees, clouds, ocean, this monstrous seething life, the same in mountains and blazing worlds. And I belong to this abyss, as do you; I spend my days pondering it!

*   *   *   *   *

I spend hours collecting bursts of sunshine in my hands, watching them flow.

*   *   *   *   *

There has to be a greater being, otherwise man would be God, the awareness of the universe, which is incomprehensible: an ordinary god, with miseries and cries, perpetually climbing toward the infinite, and perpetually breaking into bits and pieces upon tumbling down.

*   *   *   *   *

Always be good, because kindness makes love eternal.

*   *   *   *   *

Crimes of matter are punished by matter, crimes of the spirit are punished by the spirit.
   Have you ever heard of trees, oceans, or stones having doubts or trembling in fear?

*   *   *   *   *

To see the sun, the universe, to look is already a wonderful miracle. But to touch, to take in boulders, souls, to have roots throughout all the stars, in the sky and the ocean—that is the fantastic dream.

*   *   *   *   *

Man draws from himself entire worlds of beauty.

*   *   *   *   *

Man has a spark of amazing soul that wanders through the great ocean of dreams, that spreads from star to star, and everything is bursting, golden and enormous; genius, beauty, and love come into being. As soon as matter disperses, the imperishable spark returns to the ocean whence it came.

*   *   *   *   *

Each one of us creates a universe of anguish or beauty, parched or made of fire. The good are therefore content. Nonetheless, there are those that live indifferent to the universe.

*   *   *   *   *

Sometimes in the simplest of facts we find mystery. A fistful of contemptible dirt, for example, holds hidden strength. It seems lifeless. But just wait, however, for March will touch it . . . ! Thus this poor, awkward fellow, forever shy, dressed in black, led a happy life. From his dormer window he would spend hours pondering this sliver of a girl, virtually consumptive, who seemingly wore a mask on the verge of an anguished cry. Mouca was loved like the legendary princesses; the loving between the starving philosopher and the streetwalker was of an indescribable, tender attentiveness. On top of Gabiru's pile of books, someone

occasionally found dried flowers and this Spring—unheard of—
the wind brought two butterflies over the rooftop that came into
the entryway to court.

He was contented. What does hunger matter when you are
in love? Do love and faith not transform the world to its deepest
roots? Who says that marble palaces and moonlit verses cannot
be built from scattered clouds?

He would weave his ideas, his theories while staring at the
Tree. Throughout the trunk there were already tremblings: the
shoots seemed polished. Leaning out his window, fascinated, he
watched its naked branches, although bare—how can I describe
them?—clothed in emotion.

"That tree," he'd murmur, musing.

Below, the deluge persevered with tears, shouting, and
laughter: talking, trampled mud, mire blended with dreams,
no sooner born than tossed into the arena, bums, prostitutes,
monsters in whose frog-like bodies the soul of some god resides.
Why? Where? From which ruins are these beings built? Beings
destiny has scarred with tragic impressions? Made of bits of
statues and insanity, they speak in jargon. If they laugh, they
are Laughter, as if there were a sorrowful clown skipping around
inside them. Their gaze is of despair and hatred. Behold a river of
cries, no sooner born than already in pain. Does Night go about
constructing beings from the clouds, destined to end up in the
arena? Is perhaps this flowing, churning sewage—indifferent to
nature—necessary and fertile?

Every day Gabiru goes and sits down to watch Mouca among
the thieves and soldiers that emerge after dark to laugh at tears
and screams. The Old Man is always among the sinister throng,
taciturn and mean, laughing only with a sneer; and so too is the
Dead Man, who speaks disdainfully about suffering, women,
and death. Gabiru, shrunken and sad, sits down to watch Mouca
and goes about weaving his dream. The entire night is a mixture
of cries, tears, and laughter. They beat the women and when they

sob, fallen, and transformed into scorn, as vile as dirt, all the men laugh with a satisfactory—ahh!—for having made them suffer.

But that night, one of them notices Gabiru, who is off in the corner, neither seeing nor hearing, just ridiculous, gaunt, and lost in thought. He points to Gabiru and the throng immediately quiets down, tragically. And the Dead Man, placing his big hand on his chest, says:

"Hey, you!"

"Uh?"

"What do you think you're doing here, Gabiru?"

Then the Old Man opens his gullet and all the others stand up, shoving each other.

"Wait, everyone . . . Hey you, can't you hear?"

"Huh," he says, waking up, stunned. "Huh?"

Then the Dead Man, clutching his cold hands together, as if he intended to mistreat Gabiru, cries out, "I think he's a poet! They say he's a poet . . ."

And contagious, cruel laughter erupts all around, like a surging ocean. The women, used to being mistreated, consumptive, and downtrodden, "He's a poet!"

There are twisted looks of hatred; a flame, freezing and stinging. The evil resurges. They are going to laugh, to trample. Soon the chorus of laughter and yelling bursts out.

"Look at him . . . Do you know what they call him? They call him Gabiru."

"It's the spell," says Mouca.

"Look out," another says, "watch your step!"

"Huh?" asks Gabiru, not understanding anything, dizzy with sleep.

And he stares at the thieves and women surrounding him. Gaunt and trembling throughout with the damp cold, bundled in his alpaca overcoat, in the light of the smoky streetlight, for the first time he discovers the sad reality, the prostitutes, the destitute, the faces of the thieves. The faces of fear all in a semicircle, approaching him, their mouths wide open, just mouths. No one laughs at physical pain like the poor, who admire only strength.

"What do you think you're doing here, Gabiru?"

He wakes up surprised, "Huh?"

Dizzy, scrawny, and starving, he watches them. Through the mist of the dream he sees reality and, among the circle of thieves and women, he finds himself frightened, hesitant, and stooped. And around him, the others sense they will harm him. They are going to laugh at that which is poor and awkward; they are going to laugh at what they do not understand—the dream.

"I think he's a poet . . ."

And the thieves howl. Their laughter is filled with hatred; the ignorant laughter is the hatred of matter against spirit. And it has a name—scorn. The thieves and women join forces to laugh at that shrunken, stooped man.

He has gone hungry, has lived on only bread and thought, stuck in the clouds, and suddenly there he is, looking into the eyes of scorn. There are those that would laugh at pain and tears, at tragedy. Does evil cause laughter? It does. Does pain cause laughter? It does. And misfortune? It too.

The thieves and women feel like trampling him because they don't understand and they despise the dream. Drag the worst ruins and the bitterest catastrophes to a dais so that the hordes may snicker. Make Hunger howl so that matter may laugh. It laughs at everything sad, poor, and deformed—and anything as beautiful as the stars.

Scorn exudes anger. There are always cries in this mirth. Just keep laughing at Misfortune and at Pain. Transform the entire human tragedy into a farce.

"You say you're in love?"

Gabiru remained quiet.

"Don't you talk . . . ? Oh, you don't talk, is it a spell . . . ? Is she the one you like?"

"Me?" asked the consumptive girl, coughing, laughing. "Me?"—She has got one foot in the grave, downtrodden, and she laughs hatefully, for all she has suffered in life. Suddenly the laughter stops. They all have a mind to trample him, to beat him down, to transform him into themselves.

"Then, is it this girl? No? So you believe there's someone sweet on you, you clumsy fool? You . . . ! Do you all see him? I can't even describe his looks! There goes the poet!"

He shoves Gabiru, throws him on the ground, and between laughter and jeers he gets passed around like a rag. They all want to hurt him, to make him even more worthless, sadder, poorer, and more wretched, because they cannot take from him his daily bread—the dream.

"There goes the poet . . . !"

Until they finally let him be. Standing in the middle of the room, beaten, his overcoat torn, he exclaims, mystified, "But what did I do? What did I do?"

Is he going to laugh? To cry . . . ?

The laughter increases as they see him there frightened and ridiculous. The worst of them, still screaming. His anxious gaze seeks out Mouca and he sees she too is laughing. His eyes reflect the darkness he has discovered, the others' harshness, the trampled dream, left on the ground, tears, and tender wonder.

"It was you! It was you! You laughed at me . . . !" he said, pointing to Mouca.

The thieves laugh and she is the only one who stops, Mouca, who has always laughed at everything, at life, at death, even at her own misfortune.

"Hey Mouca! Hey Mouca! Look at the poet!" they all yell at the one girl.

"What about it? Leave me alone . . . !"

And she broods.

*   *   *   *   *

It's late at night . . . I go out, wandering . . . Thinking about what? Stray, incoherent thoughts: ambition, hatred, wrath. The streets are monotonous, black and muddy. And on both sides of the street, the houses seem built of paint and mud dripping from the damaged sky. What a world we live in! Ahead of me, I notice, there's an old man walking . . . I don't see him well, it's his comical, clumsy shadow I see. As he walked beneath the streetlamp, I could have sworn he had white hair. That shadow is jittery. It moves its arm, hat in hand, and talks to itself, argues . . . Occasionally it trips, rights itself, and sets off again to preach among the houses and the noise, under that drizzle, the black mud dripping down from the sky.

By now the streets are getting narrower, and I've already noted how he turns back, retracing his steps, going in circles for the past half hour, absorbed in his thoughts. The rain has gotten his hair all muddy and he's waving his arms.

From the dark alleys, here and there, night owls emerge; he looks at them and passes by indifferently, mumbling his frustrations or anxieties.

You would say the city is filled with boredom, that it's sinking in the mud. The low, misshapen clouds are shredded and cling to the buildings. The big old houses reach out heavily, enormously, and every now and again a flash of light is seen inside them. The shadow keeps walking, following along the gloomy streets. He goes along with his dream, or his misfortune.

The tower strikes three. There is a cavernous silence. The same rain falls tenaciously from the cloudy, nerve-racking sky. Beneath the downpour, the dead city is getting soaked in the mud. Underneath each one of these rooftops, the same miseries and dreams are hidden. This stone shelters hatred, crimes, scorn. The shadow loses itself in the dark, turns back, stops, indecisive . . .

What do I care if others suffer? Misfortune? The world is filled with the miserable. A dreamer who goes down? The world is filled with dreams. This same heavy sky, tattered and tragic, has always sheltered cries and catastrophes. What do I care if he suffers? Every man for himself, each and every one with his tears and hatred . . . Occasionally the man trips and falls, then he drags himself along, unsteadily.

It's dawn, and with the first light, the city looks unearthed, the houses resurge, emerged from darkness, leprous, askew, spent with hatred, with ambition, with rancor.

There he is sitting on the ground, defeated. He is all muddy and exhausted . . . At daybreak, the rain starts again and he cries.

So many tears! One day, misery, and the next, more of the same . . . that shadow is mine! That man is me!

XV
HE SPEAKS

I SPEAK. SUDDENLY my life appears before me like one of those grayish, monotonous Winter days, when even traces of the dream sleep tenaciously, the traces left by chance to their fate on the rocks. When heretofore unknown thoughts came to me my smile dried on my lips, arresting my laughter . . . Someone shakes down a tree to the end of its roots. They pull it out. The screams of the churned up earth were my screams.

*   *   *   *   *

Give me the life of creatures and things that have never been taught life. They take huge gulps of existence. Life runs through them confusedly, splendidly. What I want in the end is this: to be, to not pretend, but to be, not to live your life, but to live my own.

*   *   *   *   *

The second you meet up with your soul, just the two of you, the soul you had not known until that moment, madness strikes— but then you'll hear everything that had been dormant up until then speaking inside you . . .

What is this—scorn? From where in the world did it come? Do trees, perchance, laugh? And the mountains and rivers too? Scorn is heart wrenching. They laughed at me! They laughed at me!

*   *   *   *   *

They beat me to a pulp. What I know is learned, in vain, built of words that aren't my own. I don't know anything about life.

*   *   *   *   *

Man is only happy when he is himself. The others shove him into misery. Man needs to find himself.

*   *   *   *   *

You start out life and they will mold you: teachers, friends, books, they will work you over. Why? To make you happy—they say. Let me be miserable, have it my way.

*   *   *   *   *

All trees fill out and grow, forming links to the earth through their roots, which pierce the earth like iron plows. Mine is the only life with no roots. I have no friends, nor do I want any, and to me everything seems gray and useless.

Nature still captivates me: I stay for hours staring into a pond and I have never been as moved as I am before the most humble of trees.

*   *   *   *   *

The misery I've met with is not misery, nor is it happiness: I want to swallow bitter, mysterious, profound life, all of life. I want my share, just like the most miserable of the animals, the unknown mountains, and the poor.

Or else I will have died without living.

*   *   *   *   *

I only felt life run through me when I was young. I still recall the essence of the gentle pine trees I saw so many years ago, the untilled smell of the dew-covered fields in the morning, which made me think about the happy life of wolves and animals that breathe healthy, fresh air, and sleep carelessly in the burrows or soft shadows, and kill without remorse.

Our garden! Way up high, there's a white wall, a wrought-iron gate, a thicket of evergreen pine trees in dialogue with the ocean. Before you come inside, turn around . . . Such enormous serenity emanates from this landscape. The blue ocean and the blue sky blend. It is all blue dust. The light vibrates. A strip of beach. Out at sea, perhaps a boat, and off in the distance, uninhabited, solitary mountains covered in pines, hollowed sporadically with shadows, reminiscent of a wild, free life in a country without laws.

Here is the yard: a kitchen garden with trees. At first it seems like a labyrinth, a green flame. The collards are the size of trees and the water whispers and mines throughout, the creeks completely soak the rich, black earth. Rows of lavender, carnations, and simple roses border the planters, and at the back there is a huge fig tree, with flat, fleshy leaves providing underground shade. The entire garden, dotted with puddles, resonates like a beehive. Twinkling echoes throughout . . . throughout the solitude.

The trees were my friends there, everything knew me, and I lived a confident, strong, wild life.

Words, teachers, friends came later and I was never again to find pleasure in life, until I was woken up just now with this cry: I never lived!

*   *   *   *   *

I set to thinking: how often are happiness and misery false, not felt? Mere masks, strapped on for certain occasions because

authors, friends, and the entire complex plot in which we are
entangled teaches us so—in such and such situation you will
be happy.

And in fact, through habit, we confess—I am happy.

But take a look at yourself . . . Deep down inside, something
bitter is stirring.

*   *   *   *   *

I fled. I isolated myself. I didn't want friends, I wanted only
this: to be alone.

Why do they call me Gabiru? Shut away on the last floor of
the Building, I set to listening to everything speaking inside me.
I have forgotten reality, so that I may know reality. I threw away
all I had learned, and battled myself.

*   *   *   *   *

And now I see misery! Now I come up against misery . . .

XVI
GEBO'S STORY

So the misery only increased beneath the Building's sparsely tiled mansard rooftops, where chance had tossed them that Winter. Most days they had no bread and it was so cold they never left their cot. They were poorer than the poor, and asked for no charity. He would go out first thing in the morning, groomed and clean in his threadbare clothes and worn, patched boots. Adding insult to injury, his wife would say sorrowfully, "Come on, husband, see if they'll give you some work . . ."

"Huh? I'll see to it, I'll see to it . . . ! Don't worry, woman."

A job? Who was to give Gebo a job, injured and ridiculous, aged and stumbling, barely able to write, so blind and dizzy? Spurred on, he would get up every day to humiliation and to chase down a few miserable coins. He was virtually begging, sobbing—with his disheveled white hair.

One day he had been all over, sweating nervously. Everyone had sent him on his way. It was a fateful Tuesday that freezing, muddy Winter. He could not even walk, so bitter and exhausted was he. He knew night was upon him and it was time to go home, to his wife, who would surely be waiting anxiously.

"Well? Well . . . ? Did you find something?"

Oh, if the Lord would only help him! If the all-seeing Lord would come to rescue him from the depths of his misery! Nothing. All doors slammed shut, all souls under lock and key. Left alone sniveling, that fat, ridiculous old man reached out to a passing stranger, mumbling incoherently. Everyone at home, hungry . . . Shrunken and withdrawn, he asked someone else, swallowing his tears with excruciating anguish. Back at the garret, the two women waited for the sad, bitter bread. Meanwhile, he barely recognized the streets he wandered with his faltering steps, like a drunkard. He begged in a humble, sobbing voice, and that night—that fatal Tuesday—if Gebo still had one ounce of vanity, it had crumbled into the dirt.

"Lord help me! Here it is, woman! Here it is!" In spite of all the nagging, the three of them had a profound, admirable love for each other. In dragging them down, their misery brought them closer together. One would feign satisfaction in order that the other have more bread. If one fell ill, the others could not even sleep, until one day the woman finally collapsed. Useless, unable to get up, she whispered softly to Sofia, "Listen here, you take care of your father. Never leave his side. He has always been a saint."

From then on, no one could get another word out of her. She trailed them around the house with her watery eyes until she dropped dead. She was finally worn out from the daily struggle against constant misery, after a life filled with despair. She had been the tower of strength that had supported them both and kept them going. She was the one who fought—in vain!—blow by blow against their harsh destiny, trying to support them, grasping at the last shreds and dregs of happiness. On the days of hunger she was the first to pretend she had had her fill. She gave orders, told them what to do, went to battle. It had killed her to leave her garden trees, which she had watched grow, and the ever-trickling spring, flowing like her tears. And when she died, they could measure just how much they missed her, like trunks, now felled.

                    *   *   *   *   *

Laid out in her last frock, dressed by her daughter and Gebo, she had gone pale, withered, and was at peace, happier than those she left behind. The old man collapsed, exhausted, sobbing off in a corner. And, throughout the night, inside that hovel,

you could hear the monotonous, sad, childish noise. He sobbed
and worried, "Tomorrow I have to go find us some bread." The
same, relentless life, and now it was just the two of them, and
Misery. When his wife was still alive, in spite of their woes, she
carried on, "Next year, maybe next year bad luck will finally tire
and leave us alone . . ." And thus she had spent her last drop of
energy, as well as the ragged clothing that was so worn out it no
longer kept them warm. All hope had faded. Out of the depth
of the night, the old man would hear laughter from clamoring
mouths, "Hey Gebo! Hey Gebo!"

"Huh? I'm coming! I'm coming!"

They took her to the public graveyard in a pinewood casket
and he stayed there, clinging to his daughter, sobbing. "If only
God would take us!"

Stumbling, old, and tired, all he could do was sob, and his
daughter had to take him by the hand, as if leading a child.

XVII
WHAT IS LIFE?

GABIRU DOES NOT understand existence. His soul is like a damaged rock, disintegrating into water. He finds himself suddenly immersed in a torrid, golden sea. He discovers impetuous deluges of hatred, of scorn, the Tree, the stars, an endless whirlwind, cries, streams of dreams. To where? Where does all this flow? Death, right next to a tree in full bloom. Chaos. Darkness and sun, gushing gold, and man, indifferent . . . Facing reality, numbed, and finding himself mocked in Life, Gabiru screamed. So Winter and storms come to an end, Spring and sunshine arrive, and man never lifts his eyes? Beneath his feet the earth moves in a murmur, entirely alive and up above the foolish sky gasps, overloaded with stars—and man remains unaware? With scorn, rocks, constellations, and the deep deep sea all around, man remains aloof.

What is this? What is Life? What is this mystery where man gets caught up like a salamander into fire? Can a man suddenly come across a tree covering itself in bloom without panicking? In the most despicable of ponds the sun is mirrored, matter mixes tumultuously into infinite combinations—and man follows along his path unconsciously.

What is Life? What is Life? A soul, a dream? Does life contain reality? Is what I practice on earth indifferent or does it have repercussions elsewhere? Is this mud or fire? Appearance or some dreadful reality? And what about the scorn, and the water born glistening within the earth, love, a passing cloud, and the wind? Is all of this a whirlwind of souls, rocks, trees, of the dream? Or does this splendid stream flow to some beautiful end? Am I dreaming in a cavity, inside a closed tomb, or am I living a true existence?

And the poor? Why do the poor suffer with no cries, stirred up like the earth by this iron plow—pain? Do they come into this world only to scream?

Gabiru would observe them, going through life filled with resignation, each one bearing his cross, injured on rugged rocks, with no bread, and scoffed at. Falling down without a cry? What for, all this? Why suffer? And his entire philosophy would tumble to the ground . . .

He gathered the miserable to find out. He went to ask Pita, the Sage, the Astronomer, the others, and the poor and that night people came from all walks of sorrow and from the dream, to tell him about Life.

On their way to this meeting, Pita and the Sage talked.

"All they do is dream and then . . ."

"They're extraordinary men," Pita affirmed. "Just look . . . What is it that they expect us to explain? Life? There's already one man like that."

"The Masked Man?"

"Yes, that one . . ." and Pita's voice tightened. "In fact, there are extraordinary lands, grounds that grow only dreams. There are beings built entirely of mist, creatures whose underground soul has been created in dampness and in silence, where not even one miserable drop of light falls. So the soul grows freely, certainly pale and inexplicably shaped . . . These are the toad dreams. Toads soaked in dreams. How can you make a creature run away and flee, not from man, who doesn't matter, but from this, from living with this, this light glittering over everything, life as tumultuous as the ocean? To not see it, nor hear, nor feel it flowing continuously, all golden and green, in thousands of shapes and with thousands of sounds . . . Do you understand?"

"I understand."

"The tiniest piece of earth gives birth to mystery. It is so amazing and so diverse, like this thing you call infinity."

"What?"

"Infinity. It's even more marvelous than the marvel itself because reality is always greater than fantasy."

"Very well . . . Still, he wants to flee. I try to explain, I'm already on the thirtieth lesson . . . This man was born with a soul destined to become a statue yet, as luck would have it, he's got the body of a beggar . . . I only ever see him in darkness . . ."

"Is it horrible?"

"It is. That is why he has locked himself away to lie down and dream. I'm telling you! I'm telling you!" The Sage stopped, staring at him with admiration, "Pita, when all is said and done, you're one to experiment."

Pita smiled, all agape at the moon, and then said modestly, "Yes I am something of an experimenter . . . I'm telling you. He shut himself away so as not to feel people's pity. In the trenches you never see looks of pity, nor do you hear laughter. Everyone can forget their misery, by trying to set it on fire. His dream is underground—did you know that?"

"I know. It's like when plants are cut down, only the roots stay alive underground, with just enough life left to dream about growing and blossoming. In the tombs, they think about the blue air—and they never grow branches."

"That's what his dream is like. How desperate was his life that he locked himself away forever? Maybe sometime in the distant past, lost, he searched in the night for someone like him, so they could love each other . . . He wandered around with the toads, which only come out at night, because they are grotesque . . ."

"But toads meet toads and they settle in to talking about some star and he . . ."

"He was made to live in solitude. And such hunger! And such thirst! Water, if there is any water in the universe, which he barely knows, he wants to see it bursting endlessly between his fingers, filled with twinkling and murmurs, mountains. If there are mountains, he wants to climb and trample them beneath his feet, and the trees and the sky, and women—with all of the immateriality of a flower. Children, beware . . . ! He knew nothing of the earth when I came along. He barely glimpsed the universe before he cloistered himself away. He only knows what makes up the dream. He has voraciously taken refuge in the dream—and he dreams everything. He was still at it yesterday, if you can imagine, like a strand of gold making its way through a crevice, like a lock of May, he was startled and said, 'Maybe this is what they call love.' But that made him think about his misery and he tried in vain to break that tenuous, resistant little thread. And he finally broke down . . . I've explained everything to him, nature, life, but all he wants to do is dream."

"It's because the dream is the bread of the miserable. All creatures that suffer take refuge in the dream. To steal it from them would be worse than taking their last crust of bread. Those people are trampled in life and they dream. They stomp on us, just go on dreaming . . ."

They meditated. Then Pita sadly asserted, "Friend, we're the only ones who can't dream anymore . . ."

"No, not us, we can never dream again!"

*   *   *   *   *

There they are, together with the miserable, and they all start talking at the same time. Not one of them wants to be what he is, and each of them in their own way blames life. Some envy the sunset, some the rocks and the waters.

"Why does man exist?"

"No one knows."

"Oh, to not feel, to be like the essence of burning cinders, lost in eternal whirlwinds, sometimes in a cloud, sometimes in river springs, or in the ocean depths."

"What is Life?"

"Who knows! Maybe a hope, maybe a dream. Look at the

universe, what a mixture! Everything gets mixed up and tangled . . . at the depth of your being, what do you feel before the
dreadful universe?"

"Everything is chemistry," said the Sage profoundly.

"A dream," Pita asserted, gravely.

Only the poor off in a corner said not one word because, after
all, only the poor know life's suffering.

"But then, we're better off dead."

"That's it, better off."

They start to discuss and the poor, withdrawn, remain quiet.
Among them, diseased expressions, eyes exhausted from crying,
the simple minds, and the great minds of martyrs and saints.
Only they sense the mystery of life. Only the spent, mute and
contemplative, dive down to life's profound roots. The others say
words, fabricate with clouds. They construct.

"Life," concluded the Astronomer, "is only worthwhile spent
dreaming, taking pleasure in a great work."

"No, not dreaming!"

"I wanted to be a poet . . ." adds one.

"If I were a poet, this is what I'd want: not to write a book,
but to create a cloud . . . And have it bound. Ah, the reader, the
reader would be amazed. Imagine the colors and the dream . . . !
A cloud, just think of it . . ." said Pita.

There comes a time in life when all illusions are gone and a
person thinks about either death or crime. What we have lived
by for all those years of a lifetime seems to us suddenly black
and stinging, the book leafed through with passion and cries,
withered. The dream, exhausted. Each and every man would
kill to possess that which they had previously disdained, gold
and power. Only Pita, at one time materialistic, still defended
the ideal.

Turning to an enormous woman, white-faced like a clown,
whose name was Corsair, the Sage began:

"Only chemistry exists, believe me, Ma'am. At the bottom of
every action and all phenomena, all we find is chemistry . . . In

the Spring and in hatred. Haven't you all looked outside, where there are trees . . . ? Yes, there are trees and waters . . . Then, on rainy days the earth is like an immense laboratory. Everything is enveloped in water: trees, grasslands, and fields, all soaking wet. Oceans run from the mountains, the clouds liquefy . . . Billions of droplets. And from all of this mud, from the dragged dry leaves, from the lifeless earth, wonders are created: reactions, transformations, in a word, life itself. Haven't any of you ever seen a huge green cloud land on the fields . . . ? That's grass being born . . . And so, it is made of rain and earth . . . And from the trees—do you know?—there fall bigger drops and the smell of the damp earth and the pines is intoxicating. The tree trunks drink up, as do the humus, the roots, and the rocks, only to be disemboweled beneath the sun, in furious life."

"Well, your little chemistry," said Pita, "is important . . . but it isn't everything: infinity exists . . ."

"Where?"

"Where? Where, I don't know, but it is where that poor woman's soul lives, the one I loved so desperately, ages ago . . ."

The poor, off in the corner, listen attentively in silence to those creatures born among rocks, who have spent their life clinging to the dream. The city, misery, and the dream itself make them who they are, leaving their mark on them. What is sad is to reach the age of forty, still drunk on a fantasy, everything ablaze, and to suddenly find the truth bursting forth like a dagger. The masses laugh raucously at your poem, at the fire you've brought along with you, at your entire life. Which means if a woman came along as tempting as fruit, you sent her away, so you could give yourself entirely to your great work. You disdained laughter. For years, dangling from the rooftop, you lived absorbed in your thoughts. You burned up the best of yourself; you gave it your nerves and your brains and, when you finally emerged, exhausted, and preached to the multitudes—there it was, the poem!—and everyone around you laughed, and what is worse, you yourself realized that your blazing work was merely useless earth—rocks. In this bitter moment, your broken soul and your face took on an inexpressible harshness and sorrow. You might say you ended up with your face ripped to shreds. You start to run away from yourself. No other dream is possible for you. Only alcohol still gives you illusions, and desperate conversations, monologues, and screams, you and others like you, everyone that has fallen from the dream back down to earth, clinging to the tatters of their radiant past, which still illuminates them, like vagrants wrapping their nudity in patches torn from the sunset.

Old age had arrived for Corsair. They treated her with disdain and she dove into hatred. The Sage's theory had fallen apart. Pita was impoverished. Only the Astronomer lived lost in thought. Had they thought of suicide? How often they had all spoken of death!

"Our bad luck," Pita burst out, "is we've got no money. With some gold we would triumph yet."

"With gold!" yelled Corsair.

"The point is, my good woman, in our times, it is the sole power, the greatest force. Please, allow me to reassure you: it is God. Gold is everything!"

Each of them mulled over their ideas, ignoring Gabiru. From the building there came the sound of old papers. Leaves from trees, things rotting in the shadows wanted to join the eternal flood.

"With no gold, we might as well hang ourselves."

"No hanging. That's like a clown. Death sticking out its tongue at the living, a dangling rag . . . It's nerve-racking and laughable."

"I've already thought of that. As for me, I'd choose water."

"Horrible! Water . . . The body rolling around in slushy tides."

"I beg your pardon, in the open sea."

"A bullet, a bullet is the most efficient. And even elegant. Think about it, it's the death of lovers."

"And poison?"

"Always the choice of princes, dying of boredom, bankrupt bankers, by everyone that wants to go, but without a sound. Poison terrifies me."

They remained there awhile deliberating. What, after all, kept them living? What did they believe in? It was raining that evening, and it was a gloomy scene, as if everything pushed them toward death. Everything in life had failed them and by the age of forty, no one is reaching for the clouds anymore. Only the Astronomer was entirely consumed in dreams. The others, sensing he was still happy, dragged him down, like the drowning do to those trying to save them.

"To dream! To dream!" he preached.

"Forget about dreaming! Gold is all that matters in this life."

"What do you want, if I was born to this? I just live on my own, all that matters to me in life is to dream. How do you expect me to approach life, living in a garret, poor, and wearing a coat so worn it doesn't even keep me warm . . . ? On one side, here I am, as miserable as possible, and on the other, a whirlwind of heavenly bodies . . . So much wealth! Heavenly bodies made of gold, heavenly bodies of crime, seashores of the finest red hot sand and then the wide-open, deserted ocean . . . Perhaps heavens are trees, always in Springtime . . . Infinite worlds, colossal worlds passing by and I, poor, chilled to the bone, I understand and I see . . . ! So if I come down here, naked, life seems sad to me and I dash quickly back up to take refuge in the heavens."

"But what about nature . . ." Pita said.

"I know, I can see from my room, when there's sunshine, it's beautiful, all golden and green. I know there are trees, the ocean, rivers, but no one has ever seen them up close . . ."

"I beg your pardon, but lots of people . . . You're confused, my friend!"

"Everything in my poor mind is confused."

"Dreaming, always dreaming! I'm sick and tired of the clouds!"

"And what do you all expect me to do, if I don't know any-thing else? I don't even know how to laugh, or how to talk."

*   *   *   *   *

They talked about suicide, laughed at the Astronomer—a dreamer!—when deep down, they all feared death and wanted to be like him. To die without having lived! It was pure desperation. What they had tried to achieve, this effort to make material their very soul—which is no more than to create—had given them nothing but a freezing, shapeless block, perhaps alive, but still, a block. Why? Because their soul was thus, without harmony. That is why death terrified them, death which was everyone's "nothing," even Pita's, who was still an idealist. They knew they were to die without having lived. Life was most certainly not what they had expected: they were missing something. They had laughed at everything. Only Death was still intact, with no fingerprints left on its black clothing, with all its mystery, all its beauty. Even in men who are omnipotent on earth, death instills trembles of hallucination and fear when, for instance, the Havas news agency announces to the Earth that a Rothschild has ended up in exactly the same way as some poor devil, poet, or saint. It is the leveler, because it does not matter after all whether you go off and rot in a marble palace or in a public grave. Death mixes the poor with the rich, heroes and skeptics, egoists and saints. And from this black ocean no cries are heard, nor blessings, nor words. It is formidable, the mysterious silence. One cannot stare at the sun, nor at death, according to La Rochefoucauld.

To die, to sleep, to sleep! Perchance to dream!—Death imposes itself on man, black and harsh. Nearly always, however, under its cloak there are flashes of lightning. Nothing escapes it and if, for some, it is the mother-in-law, for others, it is the bride. At times it comes forth with fury, at others, covered in flowers, like April. Grotesque creatures, those born to suffer, slaves, pariahs await it as they would redemption. Out of so many tears, so many hopes, at least something must have been created in this immensity.

The humble, who come into this world to scream and yell, those for whom life is disastrous and who trail along to this beach, where unknown ocean waves roll in silence, these humble people see infinity as golden, filled with the light of an eternal dawn. No sooner fallen, bloodless, and without even their last shred of twisted, torn strength, they embark on vessels that await them for a marvelous voyage of dreams. For the skeptics this sea is black and tumultuous, filled with horror like that ocean ne'er before sailed, where only monsters have grown.

To them, death meant the end of life, because none of them had ever lived a real life. And suddenly, the grave, immobility. Nothingness.

The difference is simple: it is the end of misery, or the end of pleasure.

There are some pitiful poor who spend their lives waiting for death, dreaming of it. The humble, the offended love it because it is the leveler, the slaves love it because it frees them, and even those who are incomplete—that know neither dreams nor love—they love it too, because it must exist somewhere between the Dream and Love. Each one finds in this abyss that which they missed in life.

"This end, to which we are headed, almost always with terror and anguish, is it the end of life? But what about the beginning?" Pita would ask. "Philosophies and religions provide answers. They all comfort. The best thing to do though, is to follow Plato's advice: to carry you over existence, choose the best opinion and embark as if you were on a raft," he said.

Only the Astronomer could explain it to them, "Death is life—the crucible in which everything is redone and renewed. The death of any matter brings beautiful shapes, trees, clouds, colors. From the transformation of the spirit, something radiant should emerge . . .

"I've known two characters who have been preaching their doctrines to man throughout the ages: one of them laughs, the other cries. At certain sorrowful moments, sometimes at dusk, the words of one, as if murmured, dust the soul in dreams; the other one preaches, speaks between desperation and ruin. You, my friends, you know them as two characters, the Idealist and the Skeptic. They represent the two great types of humanity. Occasionally, they are confused, and merge: minds of idealists with hearts of stone. It also so happens that they nearly always follow each other, either to knock each other down or to build each other up. That is what has come down from the philosophers, whether in the words of Plato, or those of Epicurus. I really believe that when the eternal spirit needs to speak to men, it creates a voice—Jesus. When matter means to preach—Falstaff appears.

"I've heard them in my own soul, I've watched their battles inside my heart. One of them asserts, the other negates. They are the two great voices, born with man.

"One believes solely in reality, in the tangible universe, the other sets his sights much higher—on the Dream. The painful spectacle of human misery leaves him desolate, but not unbelieving: 'There, there, everything is possible, and the cries themselves are necessary for Harmony.'

"One of them is made up of sacrifice. It burns. It dies and is reborn, claiming the earth is mud, and infinity, like fire; the other assures you that in the afterlife only nothingness exists.

"And that's how it is: nothingness for those who believe in nothing, eternal beauty for those that live for it. Nor would it be admissible for thousands of spirits to have suffered with abnegation, without having created immortality. If immortality did not exist it was formed, ever since the miserable and the simple wanted it thus. From nothingness, nothing is created, and from immortality, strength and words have emerged, which have surprised men and shaken worlds. Ever since the first humiliated person has lived for immortality and bestowed eternal justice and faith therein—the infinite has created beauty."

But they heard these words with fear. This question of death, although present since time immemorial, terrifies us like a huge river bringing ideas, explanations, and theories to the surface. Its waters carry idols, religions, the purple cloaks of men who have debated, waved their arms, trying to comprehend, to see. And at the foot of this black, indecipherable figure, like the pedestal of a statue, there was always blood blended with theories, blazing coal, mud, and desperation, none of which were able to cause nary a wrinkle on its impenetrable bronze. It filled the sky, tragic and mute. And if ever a man inside that infinite caravan—moving slowly, inexorably toward death—were to lift his eyes, skeptically, desperately, or with resignation, he would always feel himself going mad with fear.

"But then, what about the dead?" asked one.

"Their dream is over."

"Who knows? Maybe the dream consumes them. They burn."

"Still dreaming. And death comes along and carries them off . . . ! What is the point of all this? Oh, gold, yes, gold children, the respectable gold Corsair, and gold Gabiru."

"Money . . . !" exclaimed Corsair, still thinking.

"If I could go deep into the earth and tear out its gold entrails until it screams out!" exclaimed Pita. "Gold is life. If I only had some! I would laugh from the top of a golden mountain at humanity and the dreams it comes up with. Trees blossom and creatures thrive . . . all this would be mine. I could destroy, build, and give orders. I, Pita da Conceição, would perhaps be elected Emperor of the World. Oh, children, remember . . . ! Evil ruling the world, evil laughing from frightening, golden mountaintops at pain, at heroism, at pity! And the young, scaling the mountain! Because, take note: I had all the children, they were all being created for me."

And, since Pita made a motion to leave:

"Wait. Where are you off to, philosopher?"

"I preach revolution. I'm going to preach it . . ."

And he leaned into Pita's ear, who exclaimed with surprise, "To the children! What a great idea! And philosophical! A great thought! Indeed, let's carry on!"

And they both left.

*   *   *   *   *

So Gabiru was left alone with the poor. They did not know how to explain life: they felt it and suffered. Standing before them, he explained, "This is what happened . . . One day they said to me, 'The treasure is here, dig!' And I started digging. Dirt accumulated on both sides. My hands were black, my clothing smelled like dirt, and I kept digging. The mine was as deep as a well. I'd forgotten the sky and the trees. One day I hit rocks, which seemed to shine like pure gold, and, absorbed in contemplating them, I forgot all about time, the earth, and the world . . . Suddenly I heard laughter outside from above. I climbed up the dirt and found myself with black rocks in my hands, covered in dirt, ugly and as blind as beasts that have never seen the sun . . . And everything was so beautiful! Everything I had forgotten, everything I had disdained . . . ! I stared, astonished, with the useless rocks in my hands . . . And that's how I wasted my life, in search of treasure I had right here within reach!"

No one answered him, only Corsair, leaning over and saying into his ear, "I know what you're about, I know what you're about . . ."

"What?"

"It's regret. You can't live life over again. You missed it. You forgot about it, dreaming . . . Dreaming . . . ! You exchanged the sun, and hatred, you exchanged all of reality for clouds! So there! You can't live life over again. Life for you was like clear running water through the hands of one of those statues you see in the fountains. It never stops, it's always the same, fresh and glittering, and the thirst of these stone figures is never checked . . . Ah, never again to have that taste of blood and youth in your mouth. The trees are not the same trees anymore, nor the laughter the same laughter. I'd like to feel hunger and to be young. You missed it! You missed it!"

"And you?"

"Me . . . ? I was young and everyone would have given their life for me. They loved me, but what they wanted was the marble of my body and my young, full mouth. The wrinkles came, my bosom withered, dried and useless, so I was shunned. And the same love still burned inside my breast. How can a cloud settle inside a dried rock? I humiliated myself, searching for love to buy. Yes! Yes . . . ! Only then did I understand that men take advantage of us, use us only to throw us away later when we have served our purpose . . . Look at me . . . I've aged. I've been living with hatred for a long time. And before the mirror, see-ing my shrunken image, I dry up even more. Scorned, I settled into hating . . . Oh, if only I could make men scream, the men who'd had their way with us, and who later laughed . . . And I dreamed . . . I'm useless, my hatred will wither along with me, unable to bloom. Useless, old, fallen. Who in the world would take my hatred seriously? Oh, what I've dreamed . . . ! What wouldn't I give to have a daughter! If I were hungry, she would go and grab bread from the mouths of the poor; if my breasts dried, she would go and steal milk. She would be my living hatred. And beautiful, so I could have my revenge. She would have to be brought up like a dream lily and at the same time, to have a soul of stone, worse than mine, more evil than mine. I would tell her everything, teach her everything, everything I know, everything I've learned from the world. I would tell her about egoism and vanity, and that deep down inside each person, all there is, is harshness and interest. Women, if they're honest, it is out of vanity, and how many of them, one step in the grave, sob over their useless virginity . . . ! And she would be my daughter! The seed would sprout, and drop into a heart harder than stone. Inside her milky body, there would be an old woman more hurt, more bitter than I am, preaching hatred to her. She would hate even me, her own mother—and she would survive on tears and cries . . ."

                    *   *   *   *   *

She left. Only the wretched stayed there leaning against each other—and over in the corner the poor, the spent, with faces of saints and eyes faded from so many tears shed. They knew not how to complain. Some of them would set to talking in a crazed, bitter voice, the voice of misery. They would raise their arms and from their fatigue and gloom you would believe they had escaped from the hospital, or from war.

One of them said, "I like to see suffering! I like to see suffering! How it spies out illusions to try and trample them down! As soon as flowers bloom, it crushes them, it doesn't like anything, not even the rush of sunshine. It tramples everything, then laughs, everything that is born, even the green tip of moss bursting through the paving stones."

A worn-out old man wearing shabby boots complains. He wants to live and he exclaims, "I was always like a mole, like one of those animals deep in the earth, digging and digging, always imagining light and never able to see the sun."

"Some misfortune and pain can be laughed at," someone says.

Someone else laughs, he always laughs at anguish, at catastrophes. He looks for pain so he can laugh and there he is, crazy, laughing and crying out, "Hey, we're trampling dirt, we're trampling pain . . . The earth is filled with suffering. You laugh, do you now? Or am I the one who's laughing?"

"We want health and laughter. I never laugh, I could never laugh," preaches a mouth in the darkness.

Gabiru feels as if the Masked Man were grabbing him. His gaze glitters with resentment and his voice, through the mask, seems to come from the tomb. "Carry us off! Show us the gold, the trees, the mountains made of gold . . ."

"It's impossible . . ."

"Oh, to never know what it is to love, to live like the others, who can laugh—and to be alone, to be different . . . I did see! I did see . . . Pita showed me and then, do you know what? I was filled with hatred. Hatred . . . No, I'm no friend of the sun, nor of the trees. I have a wound like this festering in my soul . . . laughter like the laughter of others, their laughter—and me, with no mouth to laugh with . . . This wound eats away at my life, and what a sad, anguished life is mine! I've always been sick. Even when I was small, I felt wrapped in pity. Why does God give life to some creatures, while giving others only a share of bleakness? I'm cold and I hunger for sunshine, for health and strength, and I'm constantly freezing, always freezing and unable to see one thing in this world without bitterness. I'm even envious of the dirt where rocks and thistles grow, because at least it does not suffer. Give me the share of laughter that belongs to me . . . ! If I were to expose my soul to you, you would see how it is numbed, black and shriveled . . . I've heard—could it be?— that even trees court each other . . . All I know is that there is envy, pain, and the infirmary, where even the warmed-over sun tastes like the hospital. And no one ever cared about me, ever. I would love to kiss! To have a mouth to kiss! Tell me: by any chance, is there such a thing as a disgusting rock?"

He tore off his mask, revealed the face of a tomb, with teeth emerging out of shredded flesh, breaking through the rags.

"Look! Look at me . . . !"

They left—and the poor walked behind them all, having spoken not a word, stooped, barefoot, and resigned. There were those spent with pain, those taking bread from their own mouths to share it, and those with a life of tears. They left, one after the other, without complaints, or cries.

*   *   *   *   *

Finally, everyone had gone. There was only one old prostitute left in the darkness. She was almost a thing—decay. She couldn't talk or complain. She had gone there to say *what*? What was her tremendous reproach against life?

Gabiru approached her and started observing her. Then he asked her, "What's wrong with you? What do you want? Get going . . . !"

She did not answer and he, lost in thought, went on pondering. What was Life after all . . . ? Little by little a glow made itself present in his soul . . . Gabiru, in concentration, began to dream, until at his side a hoarse voice said to him, "But why? To what end are we created? Life has treated me bitterly and I cannot even scream . . . And you?"

"Me too . . . But look: I like to suffer . . . Listen: suffering, after all, is like relighting a flame, a fire going out . . . To have a dream and to see it crushed . . . !"

"As for me, I was always like that, I always acted like that . . . Who cares? I don't remember ever being happy . . . I don't remember . . . People always laughed at me and beat me, my whole life."

"You, yes, poor you . . . And did you love?"

"I remember . . . so long ago . . . I loved. But how they laughed at me! After they had their fill, they'd beat me. I was always less than nothing. Who cares about a *wretch*? If I could only find my daily scrap of bread . . . Now it's always so cold . . . !"

"You, yes . . . Poor, poor you! I was always happy, always happy after all. And did they beat you?"

"They would leave me black and blue . . . Just so they could laugh, it didn't matter . . . And you?"

"They left my soul black and blue."

"And you?"

"I suffered."

"Well, if we've got bread and somewhere to lie down, at least we're happy."

Leaning on each other to keep warm, barely covered by shared rags, they were freezing and they mulled things over. It was a dark night, but sparks seemed to burn where they dreamed huddled up, the remains of a fire, dying in a hearth.

"Listen here, don't cry . . . Are you cold?"

"I'm freezing cold."

"Look here: suffering doesn't matter, to suffer in life, what does it matter? Do you believe that which is suffered is lost? Later the tears and pain will create something extraordinary. From all that is downtrodden, something is always born. And if you loved and they laughed at you, something blossomed, something that can't be extinguished and that sprouts with your tears and your cries. Did you love?"

"I loved. So long ago . . . but I lost everything! I lost everything! Don't talk! Oh, don't talk! Don't remind me . . . !"

"If you loved and suffered, then nothing is lost. Your hands are freezing, but mine burn."

"I'm not cold anymore . . . I just feel adrift, tiny, and lost . . . Oh, it hurts and I feel sorry for myself. And you, why do you talk? What good is it to remember? To cry? It is better to sleep, to sleep forever . . ."

"Suffer. Nothing is lost. Look: with our anguish and our cries another land is created!"

"Where?"

"A land all made up of soul is created so that later on, when the last pain with its final cries is set ablaze . . ."

"Tell me! Tell me!"

"Listen: when you have a dream . . . You know a dream?"

"A dream?!"

"A dream is as if inside our soul we had a world bigger than this one. Everything's on fire . . . When you have a dream, the more you suffer, the more it grows. The more worn out the

matter, the more it burns . . . It's not lost . . . It is built from
our tears . . . It's a palace. The stones it's built from are our
cries . . . You understand?"

"So when I loved and they laughed, my love got bigger . . . and consumed me."

"Yes . . ."

"A dream . . . !"

"Everything lights up inside us. And with each humiliation it
grows. After I suffered, I started to see what I had never sensed
before. Everything. You know the trees, the clouds, and the
stars. I see them transformed now, on fire. It burns . . . It's never
nighttime. And the more I suffer the more my dream lights up."

They were both lost, together, freezing in the darkness.
Finally, only his voice ran on. She listened to him, suffocating,
her body clinging to the earth.

XVIII
GEBO'S STORY

I COULDN'T CARE less about the banal story this shabby man tells, weakened with pain, and sweating with anguish . . . With his wife dead, his home was freezing cold. Wherever Death goes, for a long while it leaves the coldness of the tomb, rendering hearts wretched. His daughter had fallen silent off in a corner and Gebo had settled into corpulence and crying. If only everything would come to an end! But no, he had to go back to the same desperate life, walk the same streets, begging for alms to keep them going. When they went hungry, increasingly often, now there was no one there to ask him, like before, "And so? So? Have you found something?"

Sofia, who only knew anguish in life, had no more words for Gebo, not even complaints. She loved him. That old man, all white, fat, and blubbering, was her father. She hid her tears, so as not to distress him.

"Don't blame yourself! Don't blame yourself!"

"What's to become of you if something happens to me, daughter?"

"We'll be able to live. Some are poorer than we are."

"I don't think so! I don't think so . . . !"

Ever since her mother died, she had been taking care of him as if he were a child. And Gebo, his enraptured eyes on Sofia, could only say in his tear-dampened voice, "My poor daughter! My poor daughter!"

He needed his wife, who had thrown him out into the world. Many days, without frustration or shouting, he remained wrapped up in rags, lying quietly in their cot. He was like a sack of blubber, crying out, resigned and sorrowful. If he went out, he would approach everyone asking for bread, with his hair sticking up and a crazed way about him, like someone gone mad. And it made people laugh. He had lost his shyness. He would trail behind his friends, who thought him picturesque, always carping about his bad luck, distressed, stooped, exhausted, and ever more scrounging and blubbery. They made fun of him. They had given him the nickname "Hunchback," and they would ask him obscene questions, for a laugh, "Hey, tell us, Gebo, don't you have a daughter?"

And he would answer promptly, with smiling eyes, "Yes I do, I have a daughter, my daughter . . ."

"And what's she like, huh? Nice legs? Does she have nice legs?"

It was a bleak dog's life, which he could hardly withstand. Yet he carried on, aimless and sobbing. Illusions? He no longer had any, if illusions serve no other purpose than to cause suffering. When she was alive, it was his wife who dealt with the hard luck. She would wave her arms. And she would warm the three of them at the same hearth with fragments of dreams, like those who, after dividing up the last rags, bundle up with pieces of their own soul. A dream falls to the ground? Try out another dream. While all three were wrapped in the same blanket she, harsh and tense, would preach about how they would yet find happiness, and she would warm them. Those three deluded souls would stay together in that darkness and hopelessness, all three of them pondering.

But they didn't even have that now . . . Freezing cold, they no longer fell back on dreams. He cried, and Sofia mulled, saddened and lost in thought, and the two of them only shared unspoken words. Oh, it would be so good to die, to rest, to sleep for once and for all, and never to wake up . . . But, goaded on and ridiculous, that ludicrous man clung to life in desperation. Aside from everything else, Gebo was a coward. He was terrified of death.

And so they ate their brown bread, along with the tears they shed. Beneath this soil we tread on, made of our ambitions, there runs a humble river of tears, an underground river of pain and cries, which branches out and flows in silence . . .

He no longer went out every day at dawn to beg. Now he was tired, and could hardly walk. Bundled up and shivering with cold, he did not get out of bed. Can you believe he was even fatter and more ridiculous?

And how he slept! Hungry and nervous, he would fall into sleep as if into a tomb, limp, with all of his hair gone white, and his face exhausted and bitter. He never complained. He merely repeated over and over again, "I regret I've been so honest . . ."

Why did bad luck never tire of pursuing him? That needle in his chest allowed him not one minute of rest: his daughter's future. Nothing pained him more than to leave her helpless in the world.

"I regret I've been so honest."

What is the point of being good? All the bad people he had known were rich and scorned him, and the good were downtrodden. People he had saved from ruin now laughed in his face and dealt with him thanklessly or not at all.

Gebo did not understand life.

"Hey Gebo! Hey Gebo!" they called out.

And he would answer, confusedly, "Huh? Huh . . . ? If only I hadn't been so honest."

She was a sad little thing, resigned and pale. She barely spoke. She mulled. She knew nothing of life, except her family's story: the darkened home, her mother's anguish, her father's sobs upon returning home with no bread. The old woman had sometimes been mean to Gebo when she asked him anxiously, "Did you get something?"

And he, huffing, would exclaim glumly, "Lord help me, woman!"

On those ominous days she would insult life and Gebo, who did not even have the strength to support the two women.

"But look at everyone else! Look at them!"

And he, embarrassed and confused, "But what am I supposed to do?"

"Go out and steal! Go out and steal!"

It would always end in tears, with the old man asking, crazed with hunger, after spending all day long at bleak travails, "And now what's going to happen?"

The mother had a few hidden pennies she'd saved instead of buying food and, sitting around their bread, oblivious, they would talk about their misery. She would say that there was no honor in God—everything under the sun was a question of money—gold! For how many times had the old woman shared with the poor the bread her family so badly needed . . . What had made her bitter was the desperate fight against bad luck.

As it was, Sofia knew nothing about life, and so she had grown up without complaints, accepting and pure. She prayed to God every night for the old man's life, for the health of the wheezing, grotesque being who spent hours and hours sobbing.

"Give us this day our daily bread . . ."

"Dear daughter, what's to become of you?"

He had gotten fatter, and could barely move. He had no more strength whatsoever. He would hold out his hand in the streets like the beggars. They would turn him away from the shops, and one day he was put under arrest. The thought of his daughter abandoned, and hungry, drove him mad.

"I can't carry on anymore! I can't carry on anymore!"

*   *   *   *   *

The days went by, hopeless, identical, and cruel. Each day seemed the same, just as all misery is the same. Until he dropped to the floor and all night long the sound of quiet, monotonous tears filled the garret. Throughout that endless night, Gebo sobbed, prostrate. He wanted to try, he kept trying to get up, but misery had finally destroyed him: it had made him fat and exhausted, and had relegated him to sobbing on a makeshift mattress made of rags.

And thus Sofia, who watched him sobbing ceaselessly an entire day and night, all the while gazing at her; who the next day and night, with neither cries nor words, saw him go white with hunger, with watery eyes and the same anguished cry, lost in thought, and taller, walked down the stairs and entered the prostitutes' house. Every afternoon she would go down and come home in the wee hours, with bread for Gebo, who only whimpered prostrate, fat and ridiculous, like a sack of lard—and with his disheveled white hair.

Oh, the women's singing, this ragged melody is the voice of the miserable, of the poor, of those who go without bread and happiness, with nothing on this earth to lean on.

XIX
GABIRU RAMBLES ON

MOONLIT NIGHT. THE tree delves its arms into an ocean of translucent moonlight, billions of luminous atoms, wandering. It is a Colossus of greenery and kindness, a construction filled with freshness and rumblings. The solid, twisted, bare boughs intertwine where the branches split. Leaves flutter and live a mysterious, wondrous life. And there is so much moonlight that it brings anguish. You can sense the enormous satisfaction of the Tree penetrating its roots into the earth's bosom, grateful for its simple, ample strength. You nearly heard it speak . . . Listen for it in the silent, white night, filled with agonizing moonlight. Between the smallest branches, strands of forgotten moonlight stammer, filtered amid the layered leaves. The shadow stains the ground and the strands of moonlight bring it to life. You might say it is breath in movement. Outside the Shadow there is so much moonlight, all you see is whiteness.

Gabiru mulls. With his eyes open, all in pain, he lies down and still he mulls. He had always lived so anguished and poor, so alone—if he could only hold on to his dream—and he has nothing left to hold on to. Only scorn! Only scorn!

*　　*　　*　　*　　*

Moonlight strikes that exotic character and transforms him. He is not ridiculous. The moonlight runs through his eyes, his outstretched hands and, filled with moonlight, he smiles, enraptured.

*   *   *   *   *

So, what do you expect? A creature is born to misery. When she
was little, she went around in tatters, almost naked, and got her
sustenance from the thieves and soldiers. They would mistreat
her, sister of the earth, flat as the earth. She knows nothing about
the dream—can she be blamed for not dreaming? They violate
her, transforming her into stone, as dry as the stones, trivial, and
they take from her all of her hopes, spit on all of her dreams. She
only suffers. People come along to make her scream, and then
come others, and one day she sets to laughing, and she laughs,
even at her own misery.

*   *   *   *   *

You might say that over in the shade, under the tree, the moonlight builds and weaves, just as Gabiru weaves his way along.
And there is something I cannot define, something uncertain
moving—a strand of moonlight or passing wind that penetrates
the mysterious shadow. Gabiru watches, mesmerized.

*   *   *   *   *

From the ravaged earth there emerge wondrous shapes. The
more the matter is stirred up, the more beautiful the birth of the
dream. Out of Mouca's life, filled with suffering since childhood,
something radiant was created, right from the start. She laughs,
Mouca does, scorned and trampled, never having had anyone to
stand up for her, except the prostitutes and thieves. She was born
to scream—and she laughs. But nothing is lost in this life. She,
who knows nothing, tumbling along like a rock in a deluge, will
discover the extraordinary dream. From that trampled matter,
marvelously formed moonlight is born.

*   *   *   *   *

The philosopher smiles, enraptured by the Shadow. There it is!
A pale, tenuous face, where blind eyes lose themselves, a face
made of moonlight or of dreams. You might say this slender figure, thriving on moonlight, with hair blackened by the shadow,
disappears in the dark, and comes back into view in the strands
of moonlight.

*   *   *   *   *

"I created you, you're mine!" he says, concentrating, and standing up. You walk over to me, absent-mindedly, not wanting to
look at me, unable to flee from me, pale and trembling. You
come to me beneath the woven moonlight. Oh, what words
must I say to you, on my knees, exactly which monologues composed of nothing, yet great, drawn down from the Milky Way,
made up of words I never learned, nor ever knew how to speak,
but that burst from my soul like a spring! What wouldn't I give
to be the night, a tree, or the moonlight that fills me with such
anguish! I swear, the trees talk to the moonlight, the mountains
court in the moonlight. So many stars shine, lost in the sky, my
love . . . The toads croak, confused before gigantic nature and
from off in the distance, in solitude, the sound is filled with
pain, like the sighs of someone who has suffered some terrible
misfortune.

Look: I'll not sit near you, so you won't flee, disintegrating
in the moonlight. I'd like so much to feel your hand resting on
my head, so much! Look . . . !

*   *   *   *   *

Beneath the Tree—reality or illusion?—a figure is made of
moonlight, in the opaque shadow a shimmer takes shape. The
strands of moonlight come together, fog piles up, and something
trembles, ready to flee—yet alive! Alive . . . ! You might say it is

merely a smile, a very sad gaze . . . Gabiru runs and everything disintegrates . . . Only the Shadow remains and the sound of moonlight drops falling on the leaves.

He smiles and says, "Ah, that is how a soul is created."

*   *   *   *   *

Every night, very late, he goes back to the Tree.

"One is earth, the other is moonlight," he murmurs. The more Mouca suffers, the more is created here. Oh, don't run from me! Come with the night, melancholic and pale like the dead dragged out of their coffins. I made you from tears. Your thin hair gets lost in the shadow. I've never seen your eyes in the darkness, but I feel the radiance of your soul . . .

Gabiru, in the silent, white night, feels her approaching and staring at him for a long time.

"My soul!"

Not one murmur. Nightfall was mainly the moonlight. It absorbed everything. Its mysterious clarity diluted the earth and things. The pale, weak Tree disintegrated entirely into light dust. And at nightfall the opaque Shadow would also become thicker and deeper. At certain times the silence would shiver in a whispered sad sigh. It was creation! The Shadow's soul was awakening. There it is! There it is . . . !

"My life!"

He could see her perfectly. The oval of her pale face, her long black hair, made entirely of dreams and tears. Only her eyes were lost in two shadows, perhaps blind from so much crying—from the girls' laughter.

"Don't run away!"

One day he ran toward the Shadow. A full moon, way up above. The entire world soaked in moonlight was like a huge beautiful dream. The image dissipated suddenly and, in the deep shadow, in the opaque shadow, all that remained were vacant, dispersed marks, disintegrated moonlight . . . He felt the earth. There was still a sound—through the earth there ran a trickle of water, a trickle of tears.

"My love! My love!"

XX
MOUCA

IT'S A RAINY night, the kind of drizzle that muddies and saddens, like anguish. Sofia walks along the street with her shawl trailing behind. There's a glow of torches near the door. A funeral is about to start. The pallbearer's little one died. He brought him home one night, a child found lying in the street. A ten-year-old boy, abandoned with pneumonia . . . What do you expect the pallbearer to do, can you all tell me . . . ?

*   *   *   *   *

He was crying. He broke down in tears over the coffin of a boy who was unrelated to him. The man that does not even have a bed to lie down and die on cries over the bread he would have taken from his own mouth to feed another.

*   *   *   *   *

He died yesterday. Most likely, one less pallbearer.

The first waifs of the night are fluttering, this black Spring night when everyone sets to singing their dreams quietly in the dark.

"They flower at night," said the Sage.

The darkness fills the potholes. Beneath the rainfall, the torches are gloomy beams of fire. There is a commotion in the street and the stirring night swallows that hilly urban sprawl. It is the funeral. There are street women and Rata, coughing away, there is the Astronomer, and in front of the little bird's coffin, escorting the throng, there goes the pallbearer, his torch in hand, with his tall hat and his frock coat flapping . . . What are they going to set fire to on that tragic night, so muddy and rainy? Fallen women, riffraff, the old consumptive . . . No doubt, on the way back, they will all be falling down drunk.

*   *   *   *   *

Each day one of the women taken to the Hospital disappears. But they sing, they always sing. Sofia smiles, stoically. What does she have left in life? To support Gebo.

Every morning she goes up to the garret where the old man sleeps, bringing him bread, which he chews with a knot in his throat. He looks at her tearfully, saying only, "Daughter!"

Life is like a circus, there is no mercy.

*   *   *   *   *

They ask me: in which extraordinary alcove is nature going to find this fiery kindness? Which hiding place, which hidden vein? Which strength builds, which chemistry forms the deep kindness, the unshakable, inextinguishable kindness that supports and defends the poor?

The prostitutes, who used to hate Sofia, have started calling her "missy" now that they see her as their equal. They share the bread they earn with her, and when they see her down, sobbing, they are anguished because they do not know how to console her.

"She'd be better off drowning herself," says one.

"This here is a dog's life."

"Think about being hungry . . . ! Hunger is always black," another girl finishes.

*   *   *   *   *

Only Mouca still hates her. She, who was always the most mistreated, now mistreats someone else. She would trample her if
she could. The girl that everyone had laughed at, scorned, whom
soldiers spat on, wanted finally to make someone else suffer. No
one was more besmirched than she was, not because she was bad,
but because she was just like any other creature on earth created
by man for his own pleasure.

At first, they all made fun of Sofia. They felt like disparag-
ing her, seeing her cry anguished tears, to make her more like
themselves.

"Here comes little 'missy'!"

"Who would have thought it? She used not to talk to anyone,
just a little dead mouse! Serves her right!"

"Leave her alone!"

"Why leave her alone? She's exactly like everyone else."

"Leave the poor girl alone, all she does is cry. You're all
heartless."

"We suffer too."

*   *   *   *   *

They laughed, treated her mercilessly. But little by little before
her silent, deep pain, they were silenced and came to love her.
They still called her "missy." One of them wanted to comb her
hair; another, to help her.

Only Mouca still hated her, "Hey you, hey you, wretch!"

"Are you talking to me?"

"You're playing dumb. Quit acting like some fancy lady. I've
had enough. You ain't no better than me, ya hear?"

"I know," says Sofia.

"You know me? Make sure you do, otherwise, I'll show you
who I am. I've had enough. I'm sick and tired of this. You're just
a little know-it-all . . . Can't you talk?"

Sofia looks at her silently.

"Oh, so you can't talk? You're looking down at me? I don't

want you looking at me, I don't want it, ya hear? Oh, sure, you don't talk? Take this!"

And she slapped her.

"And now? Whaddya have to say now? You asked for it, you got it. Around here, you're a wretch, just like me. No little missies here. You got it? Got it? You think you're better than everyone else."

"I'm worse off." And she started crying.

But all of a sudden, Mouca cried out, "I'm sorry! Forgive me, missy! I was jealous. Get this: I couldn't stand you 'cause I was jealous. I've always been like that. Don't be mad at me. I'd say to myself, 'So everyone else has a mother and I never did?' Everyone's sad sometimes, but I've been sad since the day I was born. I'm the daughter of the earth, brought up by thieves, you've probably heard that. I've been really bad to you, please, forgive me. Envy. Please, laugh a little to show me you're not mad. Just think of it! I'd say to myself, 'I've got to drag her down as low as me. She's no better.' You know why I was so fed up? It was seeing you sad and still so nice to everyone. I'm like a dog, that's what I am. I ask just one thing . . . hit me so I'll know you're my friend."

XXI
AND THERE YOU HAVE NATURE, GENTLEMEN!

EARLY THAT MORNING Pita hauled Gabiru through a sewer that only Pita knew about, which ran from the building and discharged over at the other side of the Hospital. Pita had smashed the walls where the Tree's twisted roots had broken through.

"Hurry up! Hurry up! These roots are harder than stone. Nothing can resist them, not even granite. The Tree is going to end up swallowing the lot of us."

It had rained the night before and it was still dark when they came out of the sewer. A gust of fresh air hit them immediately, air like water flowing from rocks, always so tempting to drink, carrying along with it the life of trees, replete with emotion. They stop. A white cloudiness still floats dispersedly inside the cave where worlds are created. Stars shine up in the sky and there is the thick mist over the arable land, falling from the trees in heavy drops like a summer rain. The distant trunks are ghosts and others, further away, disappear entirely. To the north an enormous star shines. Above the mountain a huge slash of clarity emerges . . . And the tender sun, slipping through the trees, blends whiteness like moonlight, without warmth. In the furrows of the plow, rolling mist and grass revolve in the early morning—they're immaterial, as if they were the earth's breath. The birds in the thickets begin their day, singing.

"What do you feel?" Pita asks Gabiru.

"Wait! Wait!" Gabiru answers, dazed. "I hear cries and all I see is whiteness and gestures . . . But what I hear! So many voices, such a rush of words!"

"Do you see trees?"

"All I see is brightness. It's like a flash of lightning, it blinds me! But what I hear! So many cries, what a mixture of cries! Now I know that trees exist because I hear their noise and their voice . . ."

"Let us proceed methodically. The earth is here, and your feet are too. And then there's a puddle."

Everything was already filled with sunlight.

"This one dark, and this one golden?" Gabiru asks.

"Yes, this darkness spins, it's inert, yet alive. Dig your hands in. There in your hand, in this pile of mud, you have everything, particles of trees . . . of dreams, reality, and emotion."

"So this is . . ."

"A whirlpool," Pita assures him gravely.

"Is this life?"

"It's life. This piece of earth is humus. It swells with Spring, it talks. It's warm and it listens, put it up to your ear . . . Can you hear?"

"Noises, voices, the cries of embryos, a hubbub . . ."

"Now pay attention. It's always the same thing. Philosophical machinations . . . This is a world and this"—he points to a puddle—"is a world. In this puddle, right in front of you, do you see it . . . ?"

"It's gold."

"No, it's water where the sun is reflected, just water . . ."

Gabiru is slumped, delving his thin, black hands into the puddle. Then he takes them out, fascinated. The drops of murky water fall like liquid gold, carrying sunshine, a shower of sparks.

"Oh! It's stars," he exclaims, moved.

"Excuse me, as I told you, it's just a puddle, a miserable puddle. You should get used to observing."

The sun falls abundantly, it drowns, gilds, and penetrates everyone and everything. On a damp day, you hear life resurge: mud stirs, trunks thicken, and water flows abundantly on a Spring morning when everything is transformed under the sun's carpet. It had rained the day before and life erupted exuberantly,

hurriedly, even in the smallest things, in cows' hoofprints filled
with rain water; it's a life of beings that in mere minutes of
existence have an enormous task to fulfill: to love, to create, to
die . . .

"Look, a tree," Pita points out.

"It's waving its arms at us!"

"So there you have it, a tree."

"What an enormous, beautiful thing a tree is! It is different
than the other one . . . And is it a tree? A tree of water, I hear
water falling."

"It's the sound of the leaves."

"A live tree? Does it talk? It is the most beautiful being I
know. It's green, it moves . . ."

"And over there, far away, a mountain."

"That little thing? I could squash that little lump with my
feet. It's only violet. A tree is bigger! Much bigger . . . ! And what
about this luminous dust that surrounds us, what is it? Soul?"

"Philosophical machinations . . . Keep walking, look
around . . . I'm going to lie down here in the shade . . . You can
see . . ." Pita took off his boots and stretched out near an oak tree.
He took a notebook from his pocket and began to write: I owe
Dona Antónia, three months overdue—30,500 reais; Household
expenses to be received—25,000 . . . The difference . . .

Gabiru wanders aimlessly. He gets scratched by thorns,
squashes flowers and sprouts with his hands, hurts himself on
the rocks. He finds dawn-covered hedges, trees whitened with
flowers, blossoming plum trees and, at one point, he is absorbed
by an old wall, against which an apple tree shivers, filled with
flowers. Some branches seem to him to be emotion. His feet
tread over trampled weeds, which also yield their dream. He
forgets himself near the fountains, watching them gush, and he
sets to breathing deeply, wanting to drink of that enlivened air.

All of a sudden there is one of those Spring downpours,
rushed and torrential. The falling rain is warm. The plants drink,
the flowers open dizzily and hide raindrops in their corollas. You

can see the tiny green leaves grow as they fill, and the shoots, tainted with resin, crack and open with a smothered sound— ah . . . ! Everything is blurry at first, the damp earth is a huge blackness. A noise runs through the tender leaves . . . Then, like a fluttering veil, the sun once again begins to flow. The fountains gush gold, the plants have golden strands, and on the ground there are cloths and pathways of gold and shadows.

"Senhor Pita, I want to be this . . ."

"Be what?" Pita grumbles, concentrating.

"I want to be this . . ."

But Pita, buried in his calculations, mutters, "Philosophical machinations. Leave me alone . . . The difference is—22,000 reais . . . That's it . . . !"

Gabiru walks. Then he falls into the tender, new grass and lies down to watch the brushstrokes of sunshine and a branch so blossoming it seems as if it were a web of forgotten moonlight. First the trunk swells. There is something like a dark dot bursting, becoming a bud, and then a flower . . . He meditates. This day is warm and damp. The little animals, hiding away all Winter long, have come out of their burrows. Wasps spread their golden clothing on the marble of the flowers and the entire earth stirs. You would think it was alive.

What to think about? In so much silence, his secluded ears even hear animals moving all the way from the depths of the earth. They've been numb for so long they pierce their way through to the sun, they hear seeds bursting and climbing up to the light, and the gurgling, fat, happy roots as they delve into the humus.

It is the sound of a distant tide swelling, leaping, expanding, and overflowing . . . Terrified, it begins to flow . . . And everywhere the hedges, the hidden grasses, the wild shrubs no one ever notices grow. They are on the rocks, they are on the dried belly of the stones.

He walks and walks and meets up with thick, happy, rushing waters, with market gardens where greens flourish, with pine trees, and then with wild brambles—and even in the most sterile of places he finds the same life and the same love.

What is this force that moves and shakes the earth?

Is it a deluge, an underground river, white and green, that has surfaced? A colorful stream, bursting through the earth's surface in green flames, all purple and white? There is greenness so pale that you would say it is a green mist; tiny leaves that seem made of some sort of breath clinging to the trunks.

The shadow of the trees cools the stream, envelops it in a wave of kindness and freshness the trees exhale.

Finally Pita goes and finds Gabiru paralyzed, his eyes enraptured among the crushed flowers. Flowers in his hands, and crumbled flowers at his feet.

XXII
GABIRU'S PHILOSOPHY

OH, I'VE NOW discovered what a splendid deluge life is! It's emotion. It's the crystal clear vein where all thirsts are quenched. It unites men, captivates them—then egoism keeps them apart.

All rivers, like all lives, eventually flow into the great ocean of beauty. The existence of humble, simple creatures is like a current—of water or tears, but always clear. Anger, ambition, self-interest make life murky, like swirling dirt makes water murky.

*　　*　　*　　*　　*

To love others, to suffer for others, to live for others is to simplify existence, to render it at once monotonous and great; existence is made to resemble the plain, coarse blankets the poor wrap themselves up in.

*　　*　　*　　*　　*

The man who has emotions and loves is always happy. Things know him, the trees are his friends. He feels tenderness before the driest of stones.

The hateful, the ambitious, the evil pass through nature like men at war: they neither see nor hear. Things become mute before them, hold no meaning, because those men cannot hear. You, who paused tenderly before hidden, simple places, before others' misery, who were poor and went to your grave, scorned and shabby, and were received by the earth like a friend, who slept your last sleep as if comforted, like everything and everyone simple, you have lived . . . You communicated through compassion and through emotion with all of nature, and you shared your love throughout all worlds rolling through the universe, through God, through man, through stone. You knew and sensed everything.

*   *   *   *   *

That which is great is always simple.

*   *   *   *   *

Awaken the emotion inside you, so that you can say, "I have lived!"

*   *   *   *   *

Everyone ever born should have their own plot of land—their sustenance and their grave. Their daily bread should be earned with the sweat of their brow.

*   *   *   *   *

It is peculiar how thoughtless men are in dealing with the most profound things in life—and how grave in discussing all that is mere vanity and show.

*   *   *   *   *

Misfortune is always good—because it brings men closer to the miserable.

Everything in life is made simple if we are simple. Like a leaf that gives in to a gentle river drift, until finally swallowed up by the ocean.

*   *   *   *   *

Nothing in life so captivates as the great spectacle of nature: the mountains, the trees, the streams of rocks' tears, the kind man who leads a simple life, peaceful and great.

To be happy in life you must be poor yourself. To know that the bread you eat has not been taken from any mouth, nor the warm flame stolen from some old person suffering from the cold.

To be poor, to work the earth that gives us flavorful, black bread and the wood for our fire!

*   *   *   *   *

When we love, emotion flows from us like from a fountain and we become attached to others. We never feel alone: we're part of Life, part of a deluge of mysterious, splendid love. Love makes us brothers.

*   *   *   *   *

Men do nothing more than make life complicated, which in and of itself is after all quite simple.

*   *   *   *   *

The best things in life are disdained: peaceful, idle hours, to drink water thawed from snow and ice, the moments of silence when we feel God is with us.

What is the use of accumulating hatred, ambition, wealth? Isn't that all too much for one life on earth?

*   *   *   *   *

To know nothing but love—to share emotions with others!

*   *   *   *   *

To grovel! To grovel! Hatred, ambition, cries, they're nothing!
Entire lives are lost in dreams, in living alone caught up in
meaninglessness, when life is so great and so simple and comes
down to—love! Through love you know everything, even what
the wise don't know. Look at a mystery with love, and it reveals
itself immediately. Look at a stone with love and even there
you'll find thousands of unexpected things. Approach mankind,
your brother with love, even the most scorned, and in him you
will happen upon God. God lives right near you, with you,
touches you at all times. What do you need in order to feel
Him? Love.

Live a simple life, the life the poor know so well, with emotion and with your morsel of black bread, looking toward the
marvelous mystery, and you will be happy.

Work your field and, in your spare time, look around, gaze
at the heavenly vault, at man, at mountains, at love, at the sea—
and you will hear God from within, feel a freshness running
through you, more alive than water flowing through rocks.

God is so close to you—that's the very reason you don't see
Him. Just a few feet below the parched earth there often runs
a hidden vein of water. You need only dig through the crust of
the earth for the cracked, rocky ground to be transformed. A
deluge of emotion traverses worlds, men, dry leaves, and the
golden globes of the heavens!

Man has gotten himself so entangled in ambition, hatred,
and war that he has lost the meaning of life—so simple and
so great—and he no longer sees God, who is always at his side.

To find Him, return to all that is simple and great—to the
love of fellow man, and of nature, and to opening one's heart to
this mysterious fluid.

Artificial life is what transforms man. It is from artificial
life that pride was born, and ambition, mistakes, crime—and

even pity. If everyone were to live a true life—mankind would be happy. How can all of this be redeemed? By preaching Love. Only Love can still save us.

Now I see! Now I see! What a heap of infamy! What a heap of crime! Man works helplessly, in search of gold, ambition, vanity, vain dreams . . . Why? To be miserable. Harsh, Herculean work—to scream, and then find himself at the end, two feet from the grave, engulfed in uselessness, burdened with pain and shame. He never hesitated to destroy, trample, lie—in search of what he considered happiness, and which was no more than falsehood. He had no time to look at mountains, the sea, the sky—the spectacle of God, he did not see—because he was chasing after happiness. He didn't spend any time in the sun with a beggar, taking pity on his brothers, lending a hand to the miserable, because he lived in distress. Looking for what? Happiness. He never spent time by himself, never found himself, never spent even one day of his life looking himself in the eyes, looking at himself and his soul, alone with his heart. Why? Because he was chasing after happiness. He disdained everything, life, mountain air. He laughed at love, at emotion—trivialities—because tirelessly, ferociously, and marred like a coal miner, he was searching, nary a minute lost—for happiness! He's reached the end of his days, having hoarded gold and bread, snatched from the mouths of others, having instigated cries and blasphemy, self-satisfied in his pride, in his vanity—but finally, profoundly disgraced. He is two feet from the grave. He questions and does not understand. So, was this happiness? What good is all this? The poor wretch never noticed that happiness in life was found precisely in everything he had disdained!

Love, love your brothers and you will see them transformed and filled with beauty: even among the harshest, you will find unexpected things; love nature, the mountains, the rocks—and you will see a sublime spectacle; love and you will feel the hand of God resting on your brow.

Make life simple and you will be happy. Your life will not

cost you tears; your bread will not be pilfered from starving mouths. For each man that hoards gold, there are hundreds of creatures dying in anguish and despair.

XXIII
ANOTHER SPRING

Days went by, the Tree was a Colossus.

That night the Sage encountered Pita, bewildered, with his large cape billowing in the wind.

"Pita, you seem strange."

And Pita murmured anxiously, "You must have seen them. They're born, they burst through darkness . . ."

And the Sage affirmed with absolute serenity, "It was the Spring."

"Spring?! You're losing your mind, my friend. What Spring? They only come out at night, they grow in the courtyards. I run into creatures I've never seen. Some are live mud, what are the others . . . ? My friend, you could say that all dreams had come to life."

"They have. I've been thinking about this. It was the Spring. You've seen a pond, mud, and churning water? Spring comes and everything is transformed. The same breeze that makes the mountain's heart beat more strongly, creates life in that black patch—murmurs, cries, a tug of mystery. This is what Spring does: it transforms inert humus into furious life. I've seen it . . ."

"So . . ."

"So, Pita, think about it, that's it . . . All these nights, this mud created in courtyards has in turn begot these men, beggars, and prisoners . . . It came from over there," and he pointed toward the Hospital, "an emanation, the same one that makes trees grow." And the two of them shivered, shaken.

"There's something about the night that brings on anxiety . . . Oppression, mystery . . ."

"Emotion that reached all the way to their dens, where they procreate. They set to dreaming and they created. Just listen . . . Do you hear the roaring, the gurgling of a great stream, cries . . . ? It's as if we'd put our ear to the earth . . ."

"Did they create?"

"They did. What we're seeing isn't them, it's apparitions. It's what they dreamed. The dreams of the wretched have come alive. We're the only ones that cannot dream."

"Not us, never again . . . The dreams of the wretched have finally come alive!"

"For having dreamed so much! So much . . . !"

"But then, was it the Night . . . ?"

"Night. A black Spring, made of emotion and of night. They only blossom at night, and can only dream at night."

"And how did you find that out?"

"I meditated."

"They are, after all, dreams, for sure. Some look like living statues, others are deformed."

"I've seen them. It's a strange blend. Creatures of fire; others, of crime. You would say they're all stirred up, a mixture of men and dreams, a river carrying everything . . ."

"And how they must have dreamed, to make them come alive!"

"They come out of every corner. Unexpected and unforeseen. And from the darkest places, they break out in live coals. Yesterday I saw one that looked like a flower—white, all white, or made of cold moonlight."

"And they talk."

"They talk, they preach! Do you hear their cries?"

Actually it was a mixture of dreams and life. The Building itself, shaken to its foundations, wanted to create. The underground river roared with anger, it had widened, broken through into the light; the relentless sewage carted gold, like a puddle reflecting the sunset. Gabiru was preaching to the wretched. Pita infuriated him, pointing out the nearby mountains, trees,

and nature. They saw Gabiru lean in toward the wretched and
speak quietly, hurriedly, and hoarse. He left them wondering
with feverish eyes.

His words burned. And down below, indefatigable and
strong, he dug. He was seeking out hatred, stirring those words,
so there would be more fire. He would preach to them, pointing
to the Hospital, "It's over there! Over there . . . !"

He would speak about the mountains and waters, but would
get everything mixed up: that March morning had set him
ablaze.

"It's something splendid! It's freshness and fire at once, a
green blaze that pacifies and quenches every thirst. Waters flowing and barren trees speaking . . . Do you know what trees are?
There you have mountains of wealth, treasures . . . Tear them
down! Tear them down!"

All the desperate knew this character that emerged with the
night, as somber as a funeral.

"There are mountains made of gold, rising up toward the
sky; there is gold in the trees, gold in the mountains, and in the
shrubs . . . All swelling waters are made of gold. There is live
silk, and trees . . . There are trees! And so many voices speaking.
Everything talks! Everything talks!"

And the poor and the wretched, men caked in despair, listened to him and started mumbling to themselves. Gabiru's
words dusted them with worry and sorrow, and the night was
like embers someone was stirring up. First a murmur was heard,
the buzzing of the distant dream; you could then hear it rolling,
like a river filling up and overflowing.

"There's gold! There's gold over there . . . !"

It was as if a deluge of dreams had erupted from the globe.
The Building seemed shaken. That human compost had set it
ablaze.

"For having dreamed so much! So much . . . !"

What else for the poor to do except lay their wasted hands
on another universe they sensed in flames?

For so much dreaming, they had given life to the dream.

There they are, spent and burned. A log turns to ashes after it provides light, and in the cinders all logs are confused. They knew nothing in life except pain. They would wave their arms, stare engrossedly, lost in emotion as if having discovered a new world; and they would set to talking to each other incomprehensibly. They were not even listening to each other. Each one of them recounted their longings, told their soul's impoverished or golden story. Throughout the garrets and courtyards, you would find that worried deluge, crippled with dreaming. Gabiru would go from one to the other, saying words that made them sorrowful, and caused their repressed dreams to overflow. Is it true, after all, that there are trees and fountains all made of gold? Why is it that I was born to suffer? Why are there lives like those of certain seeds that never have the strength to sprout?

Touched by that black Spring, which the Sage had spoken about, they joined together to complain and each of them, by dint of their dreams, had redoubled their efforts and created an image. From those tragic, worn-out, trampled beings an apparition of strange beauty had been born; and from other mists, ghosts. They had all brought their companion—there were men accompanied by trees, by hatred, by laughter, by monsters.

"Look at them blooming! Look at them blooming . . . !"

And at night they really did bloom, and from so much talking about the trees and mountains, even the rocks smelled like plowed land.

Sorrowful dreams, crumbs, souls unable to even sigh an illusion, the dream of bushes, of rocks, of everything created on this planet that is unknown and humble.

XXIV
DEATH

OH, POOR ME, I no longer know the difference between dreams and reality. Sometimes it seems to me the Hospital itself has started to talk through its stone mouth. On moonlit nights, when everything is enveloped in icy moonlight, there it is, tenderly telling the worn, sad dreams, the dreams of the poor, the blind on the streets, humble things, nonetheless, alive, like the smallest drops of water, living only with limpets and shreds of moss, forgotten by the world, but which emanate abundant freshness.

*   *   *   *   *

They found the Astronomer stretched out in the latrine. Lately he had been hearing strange noises. Constellations of fire, worlds, and earthly things were confused. He had been gazing at the sky absorbed, enraptured, and shivering in his alpaca coat. What had killed him? Was it hunger or a dream? He went like a log in a fireplace. They found him fallen on a wet floorboard in the ignoble latrine at the guest house. Even dead, there was still a twinkle of dusty wonder in his eyes. Had he died uncovering some unknown world or discovering another dream, equally alive? And was he struck down for having seen it? The surroundings were disgusting: fingerprints on the wall, obscene comments, and amazing inscriptions. There was an allegorical drawing, a "Long live the Republic!" and a "Death to Dona Antónia!" and arithmetic calculations, a Bocagian sonnet by Pita—and amidst that mud, the dead Astronomer was like a bright constellation, shining even in the depth of a latrine.

*   *   *   *   *

A river, you might say it's a river of tragic things coming to the surface. Only the Tree grows and, as it gets stronger, Mouca ails. Her cough is debilitating. She was brought up by human misery, and she was made of the mud in the streets and of degradation. But pain arrives and purifies: it is like the fire that transforms a rotten branch tossed in the flames into a branch of the most radiant gold. Thin and tall, her eyes have a strange glow. The soldiers laugh at her, the thieves beat her, but she no longer laughs like she used to. If they make her suffer, Mouca now cries.

One day, when she saw they were beating Sofia, she asked, "And, what if we killed ourselves?"

"Shut up! Shut up!"

"You know what? I don't know what's going on, but I don't care anymore if I live or die. I've lost my love for life. Look at my body. I'm just skin and bones. Why do you think we change? Tell me: is it for the love of your old dad you don't want to kill yourself?"

"Yeah, just shut up."

"Well, this is how I am, what do you expect? Sometimes when I don't have anyone to talk to, I talk to myself. A long time ago I didn't use to remember things that come back to me now. This life is getting more and more grim, isn't it?"

"It is."

"That's right, it's just what I always say and I never knew any other. We're always born with such callings! Listen here, when I'm about to die, don't let me go to the Hospital."

"Don't talk about it . . ."

"Why not? I know only too well what's happening to me. I'm just fine with it. We all got to die, don't we? So, the sooner the better."

One night when the thieves beat Sofia, Mouca looked at

her like a puppy to its owner, finally saying, "Let's both go to the river, d'you want to? I don't care about dying. It's better to get this over with. And you? What am I doing in this world? If you're afraid of water, I'll jump in first."

"No, forget it! Don't worry about me . . . !"

"No, I won't! But of course I care . . . !"

*   *   *   *   *

Often at night Mouca was overcome with anxiety, and felt suffocated. She would grasp at Sofia, "Oh, help me . . . !"

Still, she would talk about getting cured, when the sun came back, but for the time being, everything was wretched.

"In Springtime . . ."

"Yes, in Spring."

"Do you see the Tree, do you? As soon as it blossoms, and it gets a little warmer . . ."

But March came and then April and what a transformation! There was almost nothing left of Mouca, scorned by thieves and soldiers. She even lost her voice.

*   *   *   *   *

A gloomy day, foggy, gray, and damp. The onset of night. Outside, on the street, mud and cries. Inside, the women light smoky lamps. Mouca is going to die. The prostitutes wipe off the sweat of her agony and, step by step, the thieves and soldiers come to the side of her cot, to watch her die. Her withered body molded into the sheets; and in the waiting silence all that can be heard is the death rattle, the longing of someone clinging to life and whom death is strangling—closer! Closer!

The Old Man, with his enormous mouth, disappears in the dark, and from there, his eyes shine. At the head of the bed, Sofia straightens Mouca's short, damp bangs. The sheets are soaked in sweat and suffering.

"Help her die," says one of the women.

"Is she going?"

"Shush! Talk quietly . . ."

The thieves and the soldiers move in closer and lean over the bed—Pita, the Dead Man, and others. In their cruel expressions, there is fear and terror.

"Is she still talking?"

"Shush . . . !"

They wait. And the babble grows hoarse, more shrill, as if death were closing in—closer! Closer . . . ! Mouca opens her eyes wide, framed by her sickly white face, "Missy! Help me, missy, help me . . . !"

"I'm right here."

"I'm cold, I'm so cold . . ."

The thieves and the soldiers lean their faces in, surrounding her—and little by little, the Old Man approaches the bed. Mouca opens her arms and on either side of her, the Dead Man and Sofia hold her hands.

"Here's a blanket," says the Old Man quietly. And he brings forth a tattered, threadbare blanket.

"Shush! It doesn't matter anymore."

"You might as well lay her cot on the floor, to end her suffering," the madam advises.

Mouca gasps. "I'm so cold . . . my hands . . . my face."

*   *   *   *   *

Slowly, grasping the sheet, surrounded by those who had mistreated her, by all those who had laughed at her, slowly she dies. Her life is extinguished like the last drop of trickling water. They stay there, surrounding her, motionless.

This act of the spirit freeing itself is so great—this beginning of the mystery—that even Pita looks on, horrified. Once outside, he says to the thieves, "Death, my fellows, teaches. No lesson is as formidable. It is painful and yet peaceful. Watching someone die fills a man with great ideas, my sons!"

XXV
THE TREE

THERE WAS SOMETHING unique about the Dead Man. An unknown strength—a kind of current we are all subject to throughout our lives—propelled him toward evil. His way of speaking was unusual, like that of all people that live alone and who have too much time to think.

"Who are you?" Gabiru asked him.

"I am the son of crime. What does it matter to you what my name is? My real name, no one will ever know. I have no family."

"Who brought you up?"

"The thieves."

"If you have nowhere to sleep, lie down over there."

And while the thief slept fitfully, waking from time to time only to dive again into a deep sleep, Gabiru was thinking, watching him. Every once in a while the thief woke up and Gabiru shared his bread with him.

Then he would say, "Sleep."

But that night the Dead Man did not want to sleep. Sitting next to each other, they talk at length.

"I don't know why this weather is so disturbing," the Dead Man begins. "There shouldn't be weather like this."

"Like what?"

"This, Spring weather. Even in jail, when on a night like this the moonbeams managed to get through the holes, the thieves would wake up scared. I've seen assassins shaken up. One time there was this old man who'd killed a child over nothing, just for a laugh, and on a night like this, he put his mouth right up to the bars to breathe voraciously and then broke into song. This weather takes it out of a man."

"Listen, don't you hear anything?"

"Nothing . . . When I was still in jail I met all types . . . And the murderers are the kindest."

"So, why do you steal?"

"I steal because I have to steal. It's my calling. Everyone's got one. Everything we do is written in the book of destiny. I know well enough I'll do even worse when the time comes . . ."

"What time?"

"My time. There comes a time for everyone in the world to do what they were born to do. Each and every one is born to something. There are some, for example, when their time comes, they kill. Do you think it's to steal? They kill a child that's never done them any wrong."

"What is the use of doing evil?"

"In the first place, to do evil; and when we're born to do evil, it's always good to do it. There are times when everything in me—everything!—is begging me to do some harm and my hands immediately seek out someone to kill. Sometimes I dream I'm killing. It means my time has not yet come."

"And God?"

"God created me, God doesn't care. What do I have to do in this world? Only evil. Because God created me for evil."

"Resist."

"When we're made for this, there's no stopping us."

"It's better to live with a dream, unaware of everything."

"But to live . . . ! To live with all your strength! You don't live. To die without having lived . . . ! What do you know about hunger? And misery? What do you know about being chased and fleeing? And what you feel the instant you kill . . . ? What do you know about being you? There are single moments when a person lives an entire lifetime. To live, you have to fulfill your calling, with your entire being, you have to feel as if you were alone against everyone else, and then you follow your destiny in spite of it . . . Keep going even if you crush others. Where?

Who cares?"

"But what about evil . . . ?"

"What do you know about evil?"

"Nothing."

"Evil knows . . . To have your hands bloodied and bash-
ing . . . Flee the night, your feet on the cobblestones, chased,
breathless. And then to fill your chest, your heart racing, hidden
in some dark corner or stretched out on the ground, tasting
nasty dirt . . . To not be able to breathe and have the night as
your friend . . . To be able to make people cry! To have a life in
my hands and watch it die . . ."

"And I felt sorry for you . . ."

Gabiru is thinking. The night is astonishing. All the light
melts into moonlight, and from the garret in the white silence
the mountain, the ocean, and the trees, shaped like dreams, can
all be seen.

"Poor you!" the philosopher finally says. "You are the earth,
you are the earth speaking . . . You are only the earth. I didn't
live? You're like a forge gone cold, and me? Not me, not me, I
burn . . . ! Look! Look . . . !"

He pointed to the mountains, the river, and the pine trees,
weren't they all transformed under moonlight?

"No, I don't want to see all that, it saps my strength."

"Look! Look!"

Lanky and looking like a Don Quixote bathed in moonlight,
he showed him a dream the other man could not see . . .

＊   ＊   ＊   ＊   ＊

It was that night! It was that night! Some days I feel as if a sudden deluge were coming from the other side of the Hospital. The
stones rattle, sent forth. There's a kind of link between the Tree
and everything over there. Its branches thicken and nearly burst,
and yesterday afternoon I noticed the Tree was not the same
anymore. That was when, as has been happening since March,

the sun left golden dust on its branches. The sun goes away and I swear it—sunshine stays on its branches. Yesterday afternoon the Tree seemed transformed, you'd say there was something indescribably extraordinary about it. It seemed like it was a hero or a mother. I set to looking at it, branch by branch, then the boughs and the little stems, and finally I discovered, lost and nearly invisible, the tiniest, most tender flower, so frail . . . Any gust of wind would have carried it off forever.

*   *   *   *   *

The tree shook, shattered. A live mist, a luminous deluge, carrying the first breath of the mountains, and the wakening waters at daybreak dampened the edges of the walls. And the city granite still looked like a single block, partly hidden in the night. Pita sensed something extraordinary was happening that April dawn. A gust of life was sprouting, an apparition, a dream had come true, had become real. You could say the lighting itself was tender, trembling as it touched the Tree. Enveloping it in fluid, a trace of emotion. Standing straight, enormous, having transformed the pain its roots had drunk into flowers. With a cry, Pita saw Gabiru hanging from a branch.

Ever since Mouca's rejection, he had courted that Tree, imagining some ethereal meeting, after the grave. In her last days, when death was touching her, the consumptive never took her absentminded gaze off those bare branches.

"That Tree," she would say, "that Tree . . ."

I don't know if you have all noticed . . . Creatures, even before their final agony, are more a part of the other world than the earth . . . Matter is already entirely soaked in mystery, there is more light than night . . . Things that belong to the body fall silent and, inside us, the stardust of which the soul is made begins to speak.

"The Tree! The Tree . . . !" she would say to Sofia. "Where is that born—look—what's making it shake? It gets bigger and the night radiates light . . . Do you remember last year when a little bird came to live in it? And its voice? It was like water falling . . ."

When she was taken away forever, Gabiru sank into pain. He isolated himself even more. He talked to himself and his eyes lost themselves in places she had loved. Nights already had that charm that creates distance, filled with cries, of life in the darkness, of forgotten pallor.

Late at night, at the window, the whole sky dotted with stars, he heard crying in the silence. An enormous ray of moonlight fell and the unspeaking darkness seemed to wait, listening. Only very far off in the distance, in the silence that seemed foreboding to him, you would say a trickle was still flowing from a stream—a last trickle . . . Or maybe it was the flowing moonlight . . . You might say, tears. He looked out anxiously. The Tree was even more slender in the paleness of the moonlight. Its branches called to him—and what a voice, fine and loving, what was calling him . . . ? Spring water or a trickle of moonlight?

He went down the steps, three at a time, and there he was in the yard. The moonlight had covered the Tree and beneath the magic of the night, dawn was breaking. It was filled with flowers—everywhere—and they were all like tiny little mouths calling to him, in a voice he knew.

By moonlight, in the indecisive clarity of night, the Tree seemed to him like a white ghost, vanishing and calling to him. It lowered its branches to take him; and listening to that dear voice, he passed out, held tight, dead, taken by the boughs.

XXVI
CHRISTMAS FOR THE POOR

CHRISTMAS . . .

It's a dull day of hesitant, sad mist. In the distance the naked trees do not stir. Life has come to a halt. At this time of day, the clouds trail along the rocky mountainsides. Not a cry is heard. Everything in nature is concentrating and dreaming. Nonetheless, there is a huge turbulent river that never stops flowing.

*   *   *   *   *

Traveling great distances along the roads, through hidden, silent pine forests, sorrowful old women, using an old skirt as a shawl, walk to have Christmas dinner with their children. They dodder along for miles upon miles. Their calloused hands, and wrinkled faces, carved by tears, and their sad eyes all reveal what they have lived through, days without bread, the sweat of suffering, abandonment, abuse.

The diggers have left their plows dead on the fields, flooded by rain. Everything must rest. Today's wine is comforting like the tears shed over our misfortune, and today's fire warms us like our mother's love.

*   *   *   *   *

Walking in the woods, beneath the soft, steady rain, the poor, who have no wood to burn, dig forgotten roots to use for warmth. May God keep them in His paternal grip. They leave, then arrive from far away to see their children, to sate their longing. They themselves barely eat, yet they support children and grandchildren. These old people, who have suffered years of martyrdom and hunger, say, "It's the greatest day of the year." A log burns in the fireplace. There's a snowstorm. The kitchen is black, under a bare tile roof; the blackness is cold, but the souls feel bundled up. Through a hole in the roof the stars are visible and a rock serves as the hearth. To the sound of crackling pine cones smothered in ashes, they share their bread, the sweat of their brow, and they drink wine, warmed by the trees their hands have felled.

Sitting around the fire, they do not talk. The coals start to extinguish, like a sunset, or like a soul leaving us behind. Death passes by. Through a gap in the tile roof, a star shimmers, the snowstorm ends with the sound of tumbling petals, and each of them thinks about something uncertain and vague, and far away—some moment in their life, their mother, an absent child, that dead woman who spent her days sacrificing herself for us . . .

"The fire's going out . . ."

"Put some logs on."

The fire goes out and the night shadows flock toward us, to listen attentively.

*   *   *   *   *

The poor are like rivers. They quench the earth's thirst, make roots swell and trees grow. They cart and carry, grind the bread at the mills. Thus is life on earth. All cathedrals are built from their pain. Without them, life would come to a halt.

Christmas for the poor! Christmas for the poor . . . ! How is it that these wretched creatures, in their freezing nudity, still find time to reminisce and to love? The poor share their bread, and trod upon, they share with us their tears. Hot wine! Hot, bitter wine, wine that has known anguish. They huddle to keep warm. In the infirmaries, in places of suffering, the miserable and the sick pass a long time in contemplation. The poor think about people who are even poorer than they are, abandoned homes, where the fire is not even lit; they think about a lonely, abandoned old woman who, at that very moment, sitting next to coals gone cold, recalls her sick son, her absent son . . . There are bare huts, dilapidated homes, souls colder than the snowstorm.

*   *   *   *   *

The tears shed unseen are the worst. They fall on the soul.

*   *   *   *   *

Sofia climbs the stairs with a mug of hot wine, to share with Gebo. Her face reveals enormous fatigue.

Sobbing, the old man, now fatter, his hair gone white, drinks the prostitutes' bitter brew, mixed with his tears. Then, holding each other, they weep in the cold garret. Not a sound is heard from outside, frozen things listen. They start to think about Sofia's mother, at rest in the soaked earth. Everything is so sad, days without bread, their love keeping them going, uniting them, stronger than their misfortune. They feel no hatred, nor do they have the strength to cry out. Quietly, old Gebo and his daughter weep over the woman the earth swallowed first.

"If only the Lord would take us too . . ."

And Sofia, drinking from the same cup, "Be patient, be patient . . ."

"If the Lord took us together, at the same time . . . I don't think I would be so cold."

"Here's some bread."

"Do you know what? I'm afraid to die. If I died together with you, dear daughter, I wouldn't be so afraid."

"Mother's there waiting. In the grave, there's no more hardship and tears . . ."

"Everything comes to an end in the grave. When our time

comes, misery too, will come to an end."

"Here's some wine."

Christmas for the poor, the night of communion, of tears and longing! It's not rain that falls silently, it's tears. Gebo opens the window and speaks out into the darkness with words the night listens to, with words the night carries away. Sofia comforts him.

*   *   *   *   *

Around the pine table the women have their supper. With their elbows set on the planks, they stare at the hot wine and think . . . Christmas supper! Christmas supper . . . ! Even the prostitutes want to reminisce . . . Crushed from beatings, they have curses, cries, and humble smiles. They make themselves tiny so their infamous life will be forgiven.

They talk! They talk . . . ! It seems as if the very same black Spring has filled those exploited, used creatures with emotion. They recall their life, always tearful, filled with pitiless laughter . . . One of them starts, "Won't anyone sing?"

And right away, another girl, as if her words were gushing out, "As for me, it was from hunger I lost my virginity. No one paid me any mind and my stepmother kicked me around."

"I don't even know how it was . . ."

"Well, in my case it was hunger. My dad was sick and my stepmother was so mean to me that she broke my arm because I took too long to run an errand."

"Well, for me it was real fast . . ." says another girl. "I was walking outside. Coming back from the factory and it started pouring rain, all muddy . . . ! I was cold and a man started whispering in my ear and taking me away. I don't even know how it happened . . . And did he talk! Talked so much it gave me heartache. And I never saw him again. If I see him, I think I won't even know him."

"They take advantage and then don't want to have anything more to do with you."

"My mother sure warned me, but what are we supposed to do?"

"Yesterday the soldiers beat me black and blue," adds another, showing them her sad, sore body, her blotchy, withered breasts. Her bones stick out of her back.

"When I die . . . Oh, when I die . . . !"

"Fool!"

"So what? I've got my clothes ready."

"When I left the Orphanage they tricked me, took me away. I didn't know anything. Then I started in service. They took advantage of me and kicked me out . . . After that, I had nowhere to go . . ."

"Well, I had a kid . . ."

One of the girls, who had been quiet, sobbed in the darkness. And since they all turned to look at her, she started to laugh and to fix her hair.

"I had a kid and decided to take care of him. After that, my man didn't want anything to do with me. When I went looking for him, he'd just laugh. I showed him the innocent little one and he started to laugh. 'I've got plenty of women,' he'd say. 'Get out of here!' Made me look bad. Then one day he said, 'If you ever come back here, I'll call the police.' I cried myself dry and it was all over. They're all the same. I saw him again one day, but he pretended he didn't know me."

"And was your baby handsome?"

"He was a little angel. I cried so hard, my milk dried up. We're such the fools . . . ! He got so skinny that he died."

"Maria's already given one away."

"Well, if I had a baby, I think I'd die for him. I couldn't give him to someone else to take care of."

"We can't have kids."

"I was so innocent. I laugh just to think about it! I was thirteen when I started to work at the factory. It was the foreman that had his way with me. Grabbed me, but I didn't understand what was going on and started to cry. 'Shut up! If you say a word, you're out on the street!' He abandoned me, then there were others . . . We've all got our calling."

"Here's what happened to me, I was spoiled. My father had done well . . . Later I forgot everything, otherwise a girl would die. My father was my dear friend. To do him wrong, you'd have to be heartless. And for his part, he'd never thought anything bad about me, or about that fellow who'd visit. My father was always good friends with him, had always helped him. I can still remember it, when I was sitting on my father's lap and he'd say, 'You're my little sweetheart . . .' I always had a lap to sit on! Listen here: he'd rock me like a baby. 'You've got no mother, but I'm your mother, okay?' It made my heart ache to fool him, but we did, we both fooled him. And I well knew he was married, but he'd lie to me . . ."

"Why do men always lie?"

"He lied to me all along, and I was so naive. He lied to me and to my father. The worst was, one day I got pregnant. That's when my punishment started. 'I'm going to tell him everything.' 'Go ahead,' he said. 'It'll kill him. If you want to, go ahead . . .' I shut up. But now what? Now . . . I didn't even like him anymore, I think I never really did. It was terrible. I was meant to be wretched, it was all over . . . !

"Later, I couldn't hide my misstep. My father was the only one that didn't take notice . . . And he thought I was so innocent . . . ! I waited. 'And now what? Now what . . . ?' I asked him. So I settled with my father that he'd let me go to the countryside with the man and his wife. If you could've only seen . . . ! The poor woman! He beat her all the time, treated her worse than a dog. 'Shut up!' and she would, the poor thing. 'Talk!' and she'd talk. 'Oh, you idiot, can't you shut up!' Her hair was all white and then one day I asked her how old she was. 'Thirty,' she told me, and sat there quietly. I couldn't believe it. The man would kiss me in front of her just to make her cry. He'd say, 'I'm going to sleep with her, do you hear me, old woman?' And he'd sleep with me. His wife didn't say a word. She'd cry and look at me with such sad eyes, made me feel bad. One day when we were alone, she said, 'You must be unhappy.' I cried, and she started playing with my hair, caressing me, 'Poor girl, you've got such bad luck . . . ! As for me . . .' 'Why don't you leave him?' I asked. 'I'd already have thrown myself in the river if it weren't for my children.'"

"Is there always misery? Sometimes it's better to be a whore."

"Wait until you hear the rest . . . I got my pains one summer night, in August, and the poor woman took care of me. He took my baby boy right away. I could hear yelling in the other room. I leaped out of bed, without thinking what I was doing. 'Where's my baby?' I was crawling, crept up to the door to listen. They were screaming. 'If you say anything, I'll strangle you!' that terrible man was yelling at her. 'Kill me!' she screamed. 'Do you want me ruined? I'll break your neck!' Then I heard a loud cry and it was like I was dead. 'Our child? My child?' 'He was stillborn.' The woman was off in the corner crying. And she's cried ever since."

"Did he kill him, that wicked man . . . ?"

"He did. He drowned him in the privy. Then the police came. Wait . . . the maid had heard the screaming. Nothing escapes anyone, the devil covers one side and uncovers another. He ran off to Brazil, and I went to prison, my father faced the worst ungratefulness—he couldn't believe it. It broke his heart. And then . . . then . . . We're born with our own fate."

"How about you . . . ? Can't you talk?" They asked a girl, hidden in the dark.

"They took advantage of me. It was so long ago, I don't even remember. I lost everything."

"What about your family."

"We don't have family."

*   *   *   *   *

Over in a corner of the Hospital, the old bench made of worn-out planks also sets to thinking that night. The wind had stopped. Moonlight falls through the cracks. The darkness gathers in the background and beyond, in the vaulted hallways, a lantern burns. You would say the darkness stirs. Patches of darkness tear away, fade away without a sound, through the damp, thick walls. Further back there is a kind of void, a common grave of greasy darkness. The screaming increases. Then for a few moments, the silence is suffocating, like a tomb.

"If that's moonlight coming through the crack," the bench thinks. "If it were moonlight . . . !"

Through the stairwell the infirmary can be seen, where the long line of lanterns gives off a sad brightness, revealing bodies molded in white, draped on the beds. It looks like an enormous underground graveyard.

"If it were moonlight . . . It's been so long since I've felt moonlight. It was like a white sound that used to bundle me up a long time ago, in the forest. Sometimes it snows moonlight. And there were other voices . . . You can always dream, when certain nights are born! It was different . . . There was the sound of the leaves and the wind told the branches stories from other mountains. Sometimes the wind brings news, the moaning of toads, shreds torn from flowers . . . If that dust were moonlight . . . And what if that moonlight could flow over me, warming me like it used to, when something would surge in me, mysterious and strong?"

The moans, the death rattles, and the cries intensify. The last lanterns go out one by one, as if someone were blowing them out. It's Death going along its way. Shadows flutter. The black grave comes alive, quieter, bigger, an infinite grave, to which a little light lends a soul.

And the bench thinks, "It's been so long since I've felt the morning light inside, the light holding all living things, the rivers, and the other trees, or even the sun rising in golden waves, or the green, melancholy water, flowing gently among the poplars, seemingly dead . . . I feel terrified throughout . . . Terrified? It's

like fire, except there's a chill running through me. And there's
no snowstorm, yet I still hear screaming, sighs, pains . . . If only
it were moonlight . . . ! These infirmaries also give off something
like moonlight . . . Could it be a fountain? Fountains! You can't
even recall the fountains . . . Here it's as if my fibers had dived
into a stormy sea, unfamiliar, made of screams."

The rock underneath also starts to remember and at that late
night hour the whole unconscious soul of the Hospital trembles.
It tries to recall, throbs, and soon forgets . . . The dreams of the
sick, the poor, the sad, materialize and are like clouds: they're
made of fire, of moonlight. Bands of shadows dissolve, to once
again be formed.

"I think there is always moonlight . . . and when there was
sun? A deluge ran through my body, flooded my thick clothing, and, surrounding me in blue dust, there was a whirlwind
of animals. Other trees floated in the same dust and the leaves
were either made of sunshine or else were entirely of silver. Far
away—and such an enchanting companion, always present and
friendly!—the trickling river was singing.

"Leaves would fall, floating down slowly, to travel over green
waters. Where . . . ? Underneath me, from the depth of my
roots, how many lives did I protect and defend . . . ! My roots
stirred life . . . Sometimes great rains fell, but they were always
followed by webs of sunshine, strands of sunshine to entangle
me—and the sun brings with it the smell of earth and the consoling sprouts, the breath of the mountains and of my friends,
the pine trees.

"In melancholy seasons, when water's gushing down, we're
contemplative, drowsy. The mountains are enveloped in clouds,
the earth's animals shiver, nestled among roots, and dry leaves
crackle and moan with longing as they leave us. If the mist
reveals them for a few moments, the mountains are beggars,
wearing great patched blankets. In the late afternoon, a beautiful
bluish moonlight awakens, climbing gradually, then dispersing.
It's the mist. Golden saliva shines through the water and the

poplars are but shadows. And off in the distance there was a green folding screen of pine trees, then mountains, then golden sunsets . . . Why am I thinking and wondering? I've been asleep for so long! Tonight my fibers are quaking. It must be the moonlight . . . Oh, if only there were moonlight."

*   *   *   *   *

The women have stopped talking. There is no noise. They too are dreaming. Around the table, in the pillaged kitchen, they drink the hot wine without a word. Some of them are surely thinking of a home, they drink the tears that fall in the wine, chilling it.

"My mother is surely thinking of me right now," one of them starts.

"And why didn't you go have your Christmas supper with her?"

"They'd kick me out! You think they want me there . . . ! My father, my brothers . . ."

"There's a big Christmas supper at my house. Pine cones burning in the fireplace, my little sisters . . . Oh, my little sisters . . . !"

The girl, choking, suddenly bursts into tears. The others do not start laughing as they would normally. Just one of them, sensing they were all about to start crying, sings, "If you see a lost woman . . ."

"Girls, it's our calling . . . What good does it do to cry? No one escapes their calling."

"At night my mother would heat the wine and bring it to me in bed. We all deserve some kind of life! Who can guess what lies ahead?"

"Shut up!"

"I was everyone's favorite, I . . ."

"I'm the only one who never had a mother, no one cares about me! It's all over!"

*   *   *   *   *

In the darkness, the remaining ashes in the fireplace make for sorrow and longing. They shine, lose heart, and slowly cool: lives extinguishing, a soul suffocating throughout the darkness. And thus the Building abandoned beneath the deluge seems to be thinking like the embers covered in ashes. It has stopped tragically before the Hospital, and, exhausted like a poor person at the end of his life, it contemplates its destiny.

*   *   *   *   *

Christmas for the poor! The bitter Christmas of those who have no bread and who gather, chilled, around a fire that refuses to warm; Christmas of the creature that misery has used . . . The wine freezes, the bread is hard, but there is still this one light that never goes out: "Tomorrow! Tomorrow . . . !"

*   *   *   *   *

What sad poetry won't fall like a cry onto those miserable souls, the souls of beggars, prostitutes, and the wretched!

Up in a garret, the pallbearer wants to say, "I love you!" but he has always been so crude he does not know how to say what he feels.

Inside the soul of that humble creature, naked and mocked, who was afraid to dream, and even to cry, there was a glimmer. Just like the tender amazement of a rock onto which a root attaches itself, and the rock watches its blooming the first Spring. "It was me, in spite of my dryness," the rock thinks, "it came from my womb."

Without speaking, he and Rata share their wine. He says, "We're both miserable and alone."

He hands her the wine he has warmed, with a piece of bread. She looks at it, having grown up forever carelessly, pitifully, ragged, and sad. So, did someone love her . . . ?

"Drink."

"It's so good to be together."

"We're not cold."

"You know what . . . ? Tonight I'm remembering my mother . . . Why would she have abandoned me?"

Outside, there was crying. Rata stands up and in the hallway, she sees a young girl whose mother has shut her out, and who is crying and thinking, "And what if I go drown myself?"

Rata gives her some of her bread and shares her wine and, miserable, ragged, and parched, she says, "God made you for something good."

On this earth, only the poor know how to be miserable.

*   *   *   *   *

Midnight! Midnight . . . ! In order for everything to be created, so that dust is transformed into life, what is needed? A deluge of rain, oceans of water. This is life . . . In order for something radiant to burst forth from matter, what is needed? An ocean of tears.

The Immortal spirit has been born of matter, of twisted fibers, and at the cost of cries. Throughout the ages it has grown, and through pain it has emerged. The spiritual world is now vaster than the material world. Pain is the Springtime of life. To come into life or to come into death, there are always cries. Pain plows the star-filled sky and all humble souls.

What is made from all of this? What feeds in infinity? From these trampled, anguished poor, eternal things are born— humus, fusions, protoplasm, the ethereal substance from which worlds are built. In the common grave, their tired, suffering bodies are the life of the earth: the trees, the bread, the brilliant sap. Throughout infinity, it is on their pain that God thrives.

May 1899–January 1900

Raul Brandão (1867–1930) was a Portuguese writer, journalist, and also a military officer. He was part of the group "Nefelibatas" and the "Geração de 90" of the 19th century and is best known for his realist fiction that is pervaded throughout by lyricism. He published three novels: *A Farsa* (1903), *Os Obres* ("The Poor," 1906), and *Húmus* (1917).

Karen C. Sherwood Sotelino has translated novels, short stories, and technical texts from Portuguese into English. Recently, she has taught Portuguese language and translation at Stanford University, where she is visiting scholar in the department of Iberian and Latin American Studies.